HOT MESS

LIFE SUCKS #2

ELISE FABER

HOT MESS
by Elise Faber

Copyright © 2020 ELISE FABER

Newsletter sign-up

HOT MESS
Copyright © 2020 ELISE FABER
Print ISBN: 978-1-946140-82-1
eBook ISBN: 978-1-946140-81-4
Cover Art by Jena Brignola

LIFE SUCKS SERIES

HOT MESS

NOUN

1. A disorganized, disaster at life.
2. Someone who excels at disorder and disarray.
3. A person who's holding it together . . . but just barely.
4. Shannon Torres

ONE
HOT MESS

Shannon

SHE SEALED the box with a loud, screeching roll of the packing tape dragged across the top of the cardboard, stinging her ears, disturbing the quiet of the house one final time.

Brian disturbing her quiet one final time.

But then, right on cue, her reason for existing, for pushing through and carrying on with her life instead of being a giant, pathetic ball of ice-cream-and-wine-inhaling hysterical female, screeched in complete joy. Rylie's laughter drifted in through the open windows.

Salt breeze.

A child's laughter.

Crashing waves and pale beige sand.

Happiness.

Or so Shannon had thought when she had married Brian and they'd scrimped and saved and worked their asses off to afford this property.

Work he'd squandered by fucking every female he could charm while on business trips.

Work he'd dismantled by creating a new family with a new little boy.

Work . . . he'd broken into pieces that could never be reassembled.

Or maybe that was just her.

Broken into pieces, floundering to gather them all up, even while knowing it wouldn't make one fucking bit of difference.

"Ugh!" she snapped, eyes stinging but spine stiffening determinedly because no longer would she cry over the man who'd once been her prince but had changed into a monster who'd devasted her. It was done.

She was done.

Rylie was the center of her focus. Her job, and Pepper and Derek, and her other friends in town were the rest of it.

And *this*—the last fucking box of Brian's things she was packing up to ship off to him—was the end of it.

Enough wallowing.

Enough tears.

Rylie and her students. Her friends . . . and wine.

Yeah, the wine would help.

Speaking of that, she figured she deserved a glass of red to punctuate the end of her time with The Ex Who'd No Longer Be Named, and so she got on with shoving the box out onto the front porch to join the others, ready for pickup.

She reached for the knob, balancing the box in her arms, using her foot to tug open the wooden panel, and—

"Oof—"

The box hit the deck.

The air squeezed out of her lungs.

The . . . man she'd collided with rocked back on his heels.

"Oh, shit," she said, noticing his brown shirt and realizing that she'd almost barreled down the man who was picking up the boxes to get her husband out of her life once and for all. "I'm sorry," she murmured.

"It's okay," he said. "Let me help you. Where would you like it?"

Shannon frowned. "Um . . . on the truck with the rest of them?"

Silence.

She glanced beyond the tan shirt, up to brown eyes that were looking around in confusion. "What truck?"

Okaay . . .

"*Your* truck."

He frowned. "I drive a sedan."

Her brows drew together. "How are you going to fit all of these boxes"—she waved a hand at the dozen or so littering her front deck—"into a sedan?"

"I wasn't planning on it."

"But you're here to pick them up."

A shake of his head. "No, I'm here to check out the house."

She rubbed her forehead, a throb beginning to form. "To figure out where the boxes are or what vehicle is needed for pickup?"

Another shake of his head. "No. For the *house*."

She sighed, striving for patience. "These boxes are supposed to go out today. I paid extra for them to be picked up on Saturday and shipped out."

"Okaaay," the man said, taking her mental sentiment and drawing it out one extra A. "That's good, I guess. The house will need to be cleared out for this to work best."

"The house *is* cleared out of Brian's stuff." A beat. "Or it will be, if you just take the damn boxes."

So, yes, the last was gritted out between clenched teeth.

But, fuck, *come on*. Wine was calling, her emotions were on edge, and Shannon tended to reserve her calm, nice tone for her students, not men who were deliberately trying her patience.

He seemed just as annoyed. "What *is* your obsession with these damn boxes?"

"My obsession," she snapped, taking a step closer and glaring up at him, "is that I've paid a hundred extra dollars for the fucking boxes to get the hell out of my life and. You. Will. Not. Take. Them."

"I—"

"Excuse me."

A chipper female voice interrupted, making them both turn and take in the mid-twenty-something woman in a brown shirt very much like the one the man wore. Except . . . this one had a logo of the shipping company Shannon had paid to pick up Brian's things embroidered over her breast pocket.

"These the boxes?" she asked.

Shannon nodded, dread pooling in her stomach as she mentally went back over what the man had said.

His brown eyes filled with clarity as he glanced from his shirt to the woman's. "I get it now," he murmured, stepping back to clear the way.

"Can I help you load them?" Shannon asked the delivery driver.

A flash of white teeth from the woman. "Thanks, but no. It's against company policy," she said. "I'll get out of the way as quickly as possible."

"Oh, no. That's ok—" Shannon began.

But the girl had already picked up two of the boxes and was disappearing down the stairs and along the path that led to the road.

Leaving Shannon alone with the handsome man in the copycat tan shirt.

"I'm Thomas Franklin," he said, when she turned her gaze back to him, extending his hand. "The real estate agent."

The throb in her head intensified. "Real estate agent?" she asked. "For what?"

More confusion in those brown eyes, but he answered her question.

"The one who was hired to sell this place."

TWO
NOT WHAT IT SEEMED

"*WHAT?*" she exclaimed.

"I'm Thomas—"

"I heard that part." She inhaled deeply, tried to find that patience, the one she managed to hold on to, even when her students were being extra ornery. "Circle back again to why you're here?"

He opened the file in his hands. "I'm here to sell the property owned by Brian Torres."

"Fucking Brian," she muttered, rubbing the spot between her eyebrows with two fingers. "What the hell have you done now?"

Brown brows pulled together. "Are you all—?"

The delivery driver came back around the corner, interrupting his question as she hefted another two boxes then disappeared again.

"A hand truck would probably have been easier," Thomas said, his eyes following the woman. "Though, it probably wouldn't make it through the sand . . ." He trailed off, and Shannon's gaze went to the spot he was looking at, tracing the sand that spanned the space between the bottom deck step and the concrete path that circled the house, leading to the street side of the property.

Where Brian's boxes were slowly disappearing.

"Hmm," Thomas muttered. "The pictures online showed that path looking nicer." He made a note on his pad, murmuring as he wrote, "Need potted plants for better curb appeal. Boring exterior."

"Hey!" she snapped.

He glanced up. "What?"

She glared. Her house was a cute little beachfront bunga-low. A prime location in a sought-after small town with good schools, safe streets, and a gorgeous stretch of beach.

It was not boring.

"Should we—?" He gestured inside, and she debated with herself, wanting to get to the bottom of this, while also not wanting this *Thomas* inside her house. He made the hairs on the back of her neck stand up.

This whole situation stank to high heaven.

Because Brian's name was attached.

Shit. It was better she find out exactly what was going on now.

A nod. "Let's go inside."

She spun and walked through the front door, leaving him to trail her into the kitchen. White cabinets and countertops, silver handles and appliances, a pop of ocean blue accessories. A pair of matching barstools tucked into the island, atop which sat a bowl of fruit, a princess-themed lunchbox, and a roll of tape. Aside from the lunch pail and the tape, it looked impeccable. Perfect.

Just like she always strived for.

"How long have you rented here?" Thomas asked.

Her eyes flew to his, widening, fury making her words clipped and short. "Rented?" she snapped. "*Rented?*"

"Um—"

"I don't rent this place. I *own* it. With. My. Husband." She sucked in a breath, released it slowly. "My soon-to-be *ex*-husband."

His gaze dropped to the papers in his hands. "What's your name?"

"Shannon Torres," she gritted.

He flipped through his file again. "I don't see any Shannon Torres on the paperwork—"

Shit.

Shit.

Because . . . shit.

She'd asked Brian for one thing. *One thing.* And was he really trying to sell the house out from beneath her?

"I'm sorry to be the bearer of bad—"

The front door burst open.

"Mom!" Rylie said, running in and throwing her arms around her. She had a pink hat covering her long brown hair, the ends tipped with pink because she wanted to look like her favorite YouTuber, pink sunglasses over her eyes, but her feet were bare, and she was wearing a bright pink swimsuit that matched the pink in her hair. *Exactly* matched. Thanks to copious hours of online perusing. "You *have* to see the sand-castle Pepper and I built. It's the best one *ever!*"

"Okay, Ry," she said, straightening her little girl's hat. "I'll be right out. Can you just find Pep—"

"Shan!" Pepper said breathlessly as she came through the front door, her red hair flowing behind her like a cape. *Her* hat was huge—in deference to her pale, sunburn-prone skin, so unlike Shannon's, which darkened to a rich brown in the summer. "I took this from the delivery woman after she grabbed the last box of the Evil One's things"—she started to hold up a paper then froze—"oh! I'm sorry. I didn't realize you had company. I—"

"Mom says we need to build another turret," Rylie said, grabbing the redhead's hand and tugging her toward the front door.

A red brow lifted, a weighted glance over one slender shoulder. "She did, did she?"

For the first time since Thomas had shown up at her door, the sinking feeling in her gut faded. *God*, she loved her baby, her friends.

"For the record, *she* didn't," Shannon said, then asked, "Will you be okay? I'll be out in just a minute."

Pepper froze, expression growing concerned. "Are *you* okay?"

"Fine." Shannon forced a smile. "Go on. I'll bring down a glass of wine for you as payment for that tower."

"Red?"

"Do we drink anything else?"

Pepper laughed. "No, we don't." A beat, serious green eyes alighting on hers. "Holler if you need me."

"Thanks, babe."

A nod and Pepper disappeared out the front door, leaving it deliberately propped open behind her after a narrow-eyed glance at Thomas.

See? Her friend was the shit.

Throat-clearing had Shannon turning to face the realtor, pushing her hair out of her face, stifling a sigh. "Tell me again, why you're here," she said, each syllable carefully enunciated.

Thomas set his sheaf of papers on the kitchen island and said, "I have a contract to sell this house." Her throat constricted. "And I'm supposed to do it as quickly as possible."

THREE
OF ALL THE LOW-DOWN, DIRTY THINGS

SHANNON GLANCED down at the papers in front of her and read, her horror growing by the moment.

The house was in Brian's name.

In *only* his name.

And he wanted to sell it, as quickly as possible, to upend her and Rylie's life further, to take away the one thing she'd asked Brian for.

She'd given up her half of the bank accounts, her half of their retirement. She'd shouldered the high car payment for the SUV she hated driving, but that Brian *had* to have . . . at least until his new woman *had* to have a brand new one and he couldn't afford both. She'd needed a car, and while she should have gone out and bought a cheap hybrid sedan, she'd been trying to play nice.

Which had gotten her *this* far.

All she'd asked for was to be able to keep the house so that Rylie and she could easily stay at their elementary school—she because she was tenured, Ry because she was starting first grade.

And he'd sent a real estate agent to the house to sell it,

without mentioning anything, without asking her, and she might as well admit it, without giving a shit about her, about her daughter, about the future security of their lives.

Already things were tight, since she was trying to rebuild her savings with extra money coming out of her paycheck for health insurance—since he'd taken her and Rylie off his plan—and without Brian's salary . . . *no,* without The Ex Who Should Not Be Named's income.

Yes, she was fully aware that she couldn't call Brian that in every instance. First, she wasn't going to ruin what little of a relationship he already had with Rylie, and second, frankly, it was too clunky to use on a regular basis.

Ha. She was a real comedian.

Turned out, having a man who'd made her every promise under the sun—happily ever after, safety and security, love holding strong throughout all the hills and valleys—one who then broke every one of those promises, gave a girl a streak of dark humor.

Or at least, plenty of snark and sarcasm.

Just what she always wanted.

Go her!

Shannon sighed, setting the papers aside then picking up the card from the real estate agent.

Thomas Franklin, Realtor

If she hadn't met the man, she would have thought for sure the name was made up. But, unfortunately, she *had* met him.

He'd shown her the contract that Brian signed, the papers in his file.

Then he'd wanted to look through the house, to take pictures for the listing, after which, she could admit, she'd gone a little crazy, all but shoving him out the front door and locking it securely behind him.

And she had been left reeling, a sinking sensation in her

stomach, faking that everything was fine, all while knowing she had a forthcoming search through her file cabinet coming after she'd put Rylie to bed.

Lucky her.

Also lucky, Pepper knowing something was up, but not pushing her to talk about it. Instead, she and her husband, Derek, had kept Rylie entertained, even going so far as to BBQ and make s'mores, and sharing a secret smile with each other over the tasty treat.

Shan knew enough about their relationship—and had actually witnessed Derek's proposal by s'more, so she understood the shared look.

She even understood the slice of pain and longing that cut through her.

See? She could be healthy . . . or pretend to be, anyway.

But, God, she'd yearned for that—small secrets between a couple, private jokes and sweet looks. And she'd had it for a time with Brian, she supposed. But it had been fleeting and bitter-sweet and—

It was never *that*.

Never what Pepper and Derek had.

Which is why she was currently looking at paperwork for the house, for the mortgage, and neither of them looked familiar.

Only now, she finally remembered why.

They'd bought this house when she'd been about eight million months pregnant, stuck on bed rest in the hospital, the actual papers not having been signed until the day after she'd delivered Rylie.

Her name wasn't on them.

On either the house *or* the home loan she'd been paying over the last year.

Only now, she remembered Brian coming to her while she'd been terrified she was going to lose her baby, while she'd been not living even day to day, but hour to hour. He'd said that because she was in the hospital it would be easier if he just did the mortgage in his name, then he could get everything signed and wrapped up, and they could move in as soon as Ry was born.

They were supposed to have fixed that, to sign some paperwork after Ry had come home, putting both the mortgage and house in both of their names.

And Shannon had thought . . . well, honestly, she didn't remember a lot of that time.

She'd had an emergency C-section that had taken eight long weeks to recover from—hindered by an infection at her incision site—and then when she had finally been able to move around, Ry hadn't been the easiest baby and Brian had been traveling all the time . . . and that first year was mostly a blur.

By the time she'd gotten some actual sleep, she had already returned to teaching, and then her life was a baby, trying to be the perfect wife, to create the perfect home for her and Ry and Brian, and trying to be the best teacher her crew of third graders had.

Cursive and teething and cloth diapers. Baby food, day care, and poems. Common core and journal entries and board books.

And perfectly smooth hair. Wrinkle and hand cream every night. Shaved legs. Simple, understated makeup. Getting back to her pre-baby size. Dressing like she cared. Homecooked meals and—

Years of living as she thought she should rather than for herself.

She'd fought so hard to make something perfect, and in doing so, she'd missed the fact that she and Brian were never perfect, would never be, and that she'd wasted so much time and effort and *energy* trying to make it so.

Alone.

In the end, despite the fight she'd put up, despite the effort and energy, she'd ended up alone anyway.

Shannon set the papers down, sank back onto the couch, her head in her hands, her glass of red sitting on her coffee table full and untouched. The tears threatened to come. The feelings of failure *definitely* came.

Nearly a decade, and she was right back where she started.

Alone. Left by a man who was supposed to have loved her.

Again.

"Fuck," she muttered, knowing what she needed to do but hating that she had to do it.

But this was Rylie's future.

This was *her* future.

And for once in her fucking life she could demand to get what she deserved.

So, she picked up her cell and dialed her almost ex-husband.

Ring.

She fought the urge to not hang up.

Ring.

Then, "Hello?"

Humiliation burned hot in the back of her throat.

Because the *Hello* wasn't from Brian. It was from Ann. *Brian's* Ann. Ann, who'd sent Shannon an email nearly eighteen months before filled with pictures of Brian with her.

Couple pictures.

Holding hands. Kissing on cheeks. Kissing on the *lips.*

And a photograph of the three of them—Brian, Ann, and their little boy.

Who was a month younger than Rylie.

One. Month.

"Hello?" Ann said again.

Focus. "Hi, Ann," she said. "It's Shannon. Can I speak with Brian, please?"

Silence.

Then, "Oh. Um . . ." Ann's tone was uncomfortable. "Brian and Billy are actually camping in the backyard tonight. I . . . um . . . don't want to disturb them. Dad and son time, you see."

Dad and son time.

Not Dad and daughter time.

"I wouldn't call if it wasn't important," Shannon said, stifling the sharp spike in the back of her heart, knowing that Rylie wouldn't get that. That her daughter had *never* had it.

Knowing that when she got older, it would wound deeply.

Because Shannon had lived that truth herself.

And she knew those deep injuries never fully healed, that they always ached, always made a person wonder if only they had done something different, if only they had been better . . .

Then perhaps their parent would have loved them more.

"I—"

"Please, Ann," Shannon said, hating that she was begging but some part of her praying this was some horrible mistake and that Brian really wasn't trying to sell the house out from beneath her.

He knew about her father.

He knew about her past.

He was the father of their fucking child.

So, he couldn't be that bad. Right? *Right?*

A sigh drifting through the speaker. "I'll go get him."

She winced at the sound of Brian's cell colliding with something hard, but then the noise cleared, and Shannon waited for Brian to come to the phone. Then waited some more. And even more. Then, when she was just starting to think that he wasn't going to come, that Ann had shoved the cell into some drawer to be forgotten about, she heard a scrabbling sound and air pulsing through the phone's speakers.

"Yeah."

Annoyed. Clipped. One word. Even better, one syllable.

This was the Brian she'd grown familiar with over the years —not the Brian she'd fallen in love with in high school.

But people grew. People changed. People moved on.

She needed to do the same.

"Hi, Brian," she said, keeping her voice carefully calm. "Thanks for coming to the phone. I'm sorry to interrupt your time with your . . ." The word *son* caught in her throat, the reminder so damned painful, even after more than a year of knowing her husband had made another family. "With Billy," she forced out. "But I had something troubling happen today, and I need to talk about it—"

"Fuck," he groaned. "Why is it that even though I'm almost finally divorced from you, I'm still stuck *talking* to you?"

Slice. Punch. Slam.

She closed her eyes, held on to her calm by a hairsbreadth. "Why did a real estate agent come to the house today?"

Silence.

"I asked for one thing, Brian," she said. "I gave you the money from our joint accounts. I didn't go after your retirement or alimony and child support. I took over the payments for the car you couldn't fucking afford so that Ann could have something new. A car I fucking hate driving—"

"Then sell it," he snapped. "You don't need a car in Stoneybrook. You can just walk everywhere."

Calm. *Calm.* She inhaled, released it slowly. "You promised I could keep the house. That Rylie and I would always have a home here, so I'm trying to figure out why suddenly there was a realtor showing up at my front door this afternoon."

"I need the money."

Her breath caught, that last sliver of hope that she'd somehow been wrong, that this was all a misunderstanding, died out.

"Brian," she sighed.

"Ann is pregnant again," he said, sticking the emotional knife into her gut as effectively as if he'd stabbed her with a real blade.

"You promised," she whispered, chin falling to her chest.

"We need a new place."

"Need or want?"

Silence.

And she had her answer.

"You'd really do this to me, to Rylie? Upend our lives even more—"

"You two were always fine on your own."

"Define *fine*," she gritted out. "Because I thought I was pulling my weight in a relationship where my husband was working just hard as I was, rather than sticking his fucking dick in a woman and knocking her up when we were trying to make our own kid—"

"Not this again," he muttered.

"No. *No*," she said, voice going cold. "You don't get to do this to me again. This is *not* my fault—"

"You had such a stranglehold on every part of our lives, Shannon," he interrupted. "I couldn't keep living like that."

"Then why didn't you just say something?" she screeched. "Why—" She caught herself, forced her voice to lower so she didn't wake Rylie. "Why didn't you just end things between us?"

A beat.

"Because I couldn't handle you looking like the same beat-up puppy as you did when your dad left."

The air froze in her lungs.

"It was already bad enough that the few days I'd be home, you were trying so fucking hard." She could imagine his lips curving up into a smirk. "God, it was so fucking pathetic—"

She swallowed the pain, pushed down the hurt.

The good thing—and the *only* good thing about her marriage, aside from Rylie—was that Shannon had gotten really good at compartmentalizing things.

So, she locked up Brian's words and focused on what was really important.

"I need you to call off your realtor," she said firmly. "And I need you and I to take care of getting the house in my name. I need that to happen or I won't sign the final divorce paperwork, and I *will* have my attorney go after you for both alimony and child support."

He scoffed. "You think you're so smart, don't you?" he sneered. "You've always thought you were better than everyone."

Shan's jaw dropped open because that was about as far from the truth as anyone had ever come up with. Her struggle for her entire life had been trying to find a way to please her father, for him to be proud of her, and then transitioning that same battle over to Brian when they'd begun dating, when they'd eventually married.

Every action had been carefully crafted and thought out, trying not to misstep. Trying to make sure everyone liked her.

"Well," Brian went on before she could tell him that—not that he'd listen, anyway. He was too far gone detailing how wrong she was about everything. "You can try and go after me, or contest the divorce, but I think you'll find that because the settlement has been agreed upon by the court—"

"The settlement said that I'm getting the house."

"No," he said, and the *gotcha* moment seemed to ring through the airwaves with crystal clarity. "We agreed you'd keep the assets in your name, and I would keep those in my name."

Ice slid down her spine. "The house—"

"Is in my name."

"Don't do this, Brian," she said. "Please—"

A voice rang in the background, calling out, "Dad!"

"I need to go."

"Brian—"

Click.

He hung up.

And when she called back, he didn't pick up.

Shannon sat on the couch for a long time, the sky darkening, her heart wrenching, aching, throbbing for her daughter. For herself.

She'd given everything to Brian.

And just like life liked to prove to her time and time *and* time again, giving everything didn't matter in the least.

Because men didn't take care with the gifts that were given.

Men didn't give a fuck about the hearts passed over on a silver platter.

They took and took and *took*, until she was simply a shell of herself.

She'd thought Brian was different.

Oh, how wrong she'd been.

And now, her daughter was going to pay the price for her naïveté.

SHE WAS SUPPOSED to be making lesson plans.

Instead, she was sitting in her lawyer's office.

"The house isn't in both of your names?" he asked, and the horror in his expression made the knot in Shannon's gut tighten and sink even lower.

"No," she said and explained about the difficult pregnancy, about the bed rest and timing of when the house had closed. But as she talked, as she told Alberto more details, the expression on his face didn't give her comfort.

In fact, it made Shan feel like she was in deep shit.

Deep shit that was getting deeper by the second.

When she'd finished with her explanation, Alberto sat back and steepled his fingers under his chin. "I wish I'd know this before."

"I-I forgot," she whispered. "Until the realtor showed up— I — It hadn't crossed my mind." A shake of her head. "I had Rylie, and we were so busy, and I was working, and Brian was never—"

She swallowed the rest of her words.

"I'm sure I can get you half of the profits from the sale of the house," he said, making notes on a legal pad in front of him. "It was an asset acquired during your marriage. I might even be able to go back and secure some child support for Rylie, half of what you've been paying for the mortgage over the last year, but if Brian is being honest about his funds being short, then we might have a hard time collecting."

"I don't want half of its value," she whispered. "I just want the house. I—I worked so damned hard to make it a home for Ry and me. It's the one place—" She cut herself off again. "The court doesn't care about that, do they?"

Alberto sighed. "It's a toss-up. They want to keep kids secure, but you should consider that half of the proceeds *could* get you a very nice place in one of the nearby towns. It wouldn't be beachfront, but it would be in a safe neighborhood and with good schools."

"Ry is already in a good school—" A shake of her head. "And my job—"

He touched her hand. "I get it," he said. "I really do know how important the house is to you, and I'll do my best to keep it for you."

"Why do I feel like there's a *but* attached to that sentence?"

"Because there is," he murmured.

Fuck.

"I'll try. I just . . . I have to tell you that I don't know if I'll succeed."

Shannon's eyes slid closed. "Okay," she whispered then sighed and stood. "Thanks for seeing me on such short notice."

"I'm here for you."

Another man.

Another promise.

Another assurance that she didn't think would be kept.

FOUR
SAND TOYS LEAD TO A GUT PUNCH

Finn

HE KNOCKED on the door of the cute little bungalow that was next to his, a pail of sand toys in his hand. It was around lunchtime, and he was met with an adorable face peeking through the glass panel, its paisley curtain shoved carelessly to the side.

Freckles on a nose.

Eyes more brown than blue.

"Mom!" she yelled. "It's a man!"

"Grab your book and take it onto the deck, honey. You need to finish up your summer reading," came a female voice—not yelling, but still clearly heard because the windows along the front of the house were open to let in the fresh ocean air.

The little girl made a face but stepped back from the door, and Finn heard the pounding of footsteps on the floor.

A few seconds later, the knob turned, and a woman stood in front of him.

Gut punch.

The pain in her eyes was a fist to the stomach, hurting like hell, stealing his breath, burning through him.

And yet, she was beautiful.

Not a hair out of place. Her body was clad in a pretty blouse and form-fitting jeans, but with bare feet, a pop of red on her toes, on her lips. She looked more model than mom in the pale pink silk with long, dark hair flowing down her back in shining waves. His fingers itched to stroke, if only to prove to himself that the locks would be as soft as they looked. A cluster of bracelets on her arm clinked together as she lifted a hand, shielding her startling blue eyes from the sun.

Insane.

He saw beauty all the time, worked with some of the most beautiful females on the planet. That this woman should arrest some part of him, render him frozen in inaction just staring at her, when he was quite literally trained to always have a sound-bite, to always be charming—

He was literally losing his mind.

But then again, that was why he was here, wasn't it?

Well, not in front of this actual house, but in Stoneybrook in the first place.

An actor has one meltdown . . .

"Hi," she said, startling blue eyes careful. "Are you . . . um . . . new in town?"

He opened his mouth, holding up the bucket, when the little girl he'd seen in the window came barreling through, book clutched in one hand, stuffed fox in the other, and nearly knocking him over.

The girl was fast *and* strong.

"Whoa," he said, rocking back.

"Sorry!" she called, skidding her way to a deck chair.

"Rylie."

Just her name. In a tone that brokered no argument, but wasn't raised in volume or tinted with anger.

Model. Mom. Superhero.

This woman could be all three.

Rylie stopped, set her things down, then came over wearing a guilty expression on her face. "I'm sorry I ran into you, Mr.—"

"Stoneman," he said, filling in the blank and not considering that it was bad for him to have given his real name when he was supposed to be in the tiny East Coast town hiding and quote-unquote-finding himself while on his break for 'exhaustion' (direct quote there, from his publicist). "Finn Stoneman."

"Mr. Stoneman," Rylie repeated.

He glanced from the eyes beneath him—blue with streaks of brown—to those next to him—the arresting clear blue of a summer's sky—and hesitated for a moment, not sure what to say. But there wasn't any recognition in the mom-slash-model-slash-superhero's eyes—and not to be an arrogant asshole, but how was that even possible with his face on every magazine, every news site, every morning TV show? When his name had carried many of the big blockbuster films of the last decade? Still, he figured he'd better get his shit together and stop thinking so hard, because if Rylie was anything like his nieces and nephews, then he would only have her attention for another zero-point-three seconds.

So, he crouched down, met her gaze straight on, and said, "Thanks for apologizing. I'm not hurt."

Clunky, definitely.

But his sister hated when someone told her kids, "It's okay," when she corrected them for their behavior, saying it undermined what they could learn in that moment.

Whether or not he agreed with his sister wasn't in question —though, for the record, he thought she made a valuable point—

one he'd taken, promising himself he'd make sure to use the knowledge for good.

Rylie glanced at her mother, who nodded with an encouraging smile, then ran back over to the chair, picked up her book, and started reading.

"Thanks for that," she murmured, still no recognition, which was just . . . ego popping? Amazing? Confusing? A breath of fresh air? Finn had constantly been recognized everywhere he went for years now, and he didn't quite know how to respond to someone not knowing who he was.

So, yeah, ego-diminishing.

"She's a ball of energy sometimes," the woman murmured, eyes on her daughter, "and hasn't quite learned to control her body. Thank you for being so great with her."

Finn smiled. "My nieces and nephews are the same. Tiny maniacs, the lot of them."

Her expression warmed. "Oh?"

"I'm one of five kids," he told her. "The middle child with both a sister and brother on either side of me. Only my older siblings have kids though. A *lot* of them."

"Define a *lot*."

He grinned.

"I have four nephews and two nieces, ranging from ten to three."

"Okay." Her brows lifted. "That is . . ."

"A lot?" he teased and grinned. "You should see us at our family dinners." He laughed. "I swear, my parents' neighbors would hate us if they weren't invited to eat the feast my mom cooks up every Sunday."

"*Every* Sunday?" Her eyes widened.

Finn laughed. "I can tell by your face that you think it's a lot," he teased. "And you'd be right. It *is* a lot. But they're my family, and I love them." A beat. "Plus, not all of us always get together. Whoever's in town or not busy heads over to my parents and we just . . . hang out as a family."

"That's wonderful," this woman murmured, but the tone was off. And when he looked at her face, the pain in her eyes stole his breath. But then she was smiling, and it was gone—or maybe not gone so much as tucked carefully away.

"I'm sorry," she said with a sharp shake of her head. "I didn't even ask. How can I help you?"

Finn blinked, forced himself to focus on why he'd meandered over to this house in the first place, or at least on the reason he was telling himself he'd come over—that he most definitely *wasn't* lonely after having spent too much of the last years surrounded by people, but rather, was just trying to be a good neighbor. He held up the bucket inscribed with the name *Rylie* on it. "I found this on my deck. Wasn't sure if it had been misplaced or left behind, but I saw the toys on your deck and thought, perhaps, it might belong here."

"Left behind?"

"I'm renting the house next door." He pointed behind him to the small cottage that mirrored hers, one of a few houses lined up along the beach, their front doors facing the ocean. "Just for the summer." He waved the bucket slightly, the plastic shovel rattling. "I'm guessing there's only one Rylie in these parts."

"You've guessed right," she said, taking it from him, slipping beside him and out the front door to set it down in a large tub that held a gaggle of other beach toys. Less than a foot separated them, and he could smell the sweet floral notes of her hair, feel the heat of her body. Or maybe that was just him and more insanity.

He'd gone more than a year without feeling a lick of desire.

One glimpse of *this* woman, of her sad eyes, her sweet scent, and his cock twitched.

He wanted.

For the first time in as long as he could remember.

"Sorry it was left on your deck," she murmured, drawing him back into the conversation. "Rylie and the little girl who stayed there a few weeks earlier this summer were thick as thieves." Her mouth curved. "If you find any rogue toys, then *that* little one"—she pointed to her daughter, cuddled up with her stuffed animal, eyes on the page—"is probably the culprit."

Finn chuckled. "Noted. I'll be sure to storm over if I step on a Lego."

"Ah, you joke, but you must not have suffered that particular parental torture if you can make light of it." Her smile made his breath catch again.

She was . . . incredible.

Sweet. Lovely. Beautiful. And . . . sad.

So, *so* sad.

Her gaze met his, and he went rigid, hating the fact she was sad, this woman he didn't know from a stranger was in pain, and yet wondering how the rest of the world didn't see it, because otherwise they would want to storm in and take away that hurt.

But . . . he wasn't here for that.

He was messed up, and bringing his special brand of *messed up* into this woman's life wasn't an option. "I'm just going to go."

Sad got sadder.

And . . . *fuck.*

"Of course." She stepped back. "Thanks again."

Dark brown hair that shone in the afternoon sunlight, skin a deep gold that made the turquoise of her eyes stand out in sharp relief, lush, pink lips.

That parted.

That tipped up into a smile.

One that didn't reach her eyes. *Again.*

And even though he didn't know her, even though he was just going to be in town for a couple of months, *even though* she was only a temporary next-door neighbor—albeit one who seemed lovely and had an adorable kid—Finn made himself a promise.

In *that* moment, he made it his mission that if he did *nothing* else in his time away from Hollywood, then he would get this woman to smile for real.

Not just with her lips, but with her eyes.

With her heart.

He turned away, stopped, then spun back around to face her. "What's your name?"

"I'm Shannon," she murmured, extending a hand for him to shake.

His fingers met hers, his palm collided with hers, and . . . *sparks*, heat licking up his arm, consuming him with desire.

And Finn, who hadn't felt anything real in far too long—

His skin prickled, his cock twitched, and . . . his *heart* pulsed.

FIVE
GRACEFUL AS AN ELEPHANT ON ROLLERBLADES

Shannon

SHE WATCHED THE TALL, gorgeous man walk away, his stride loose-limbed and familiar, but her mind was too clouded with everything that had happened since the damn realtor had shown up at her front door, since Brian had screwed her over. Again. Worse, she felt beyond dumb for letting it happen, for holding on to stupid hope that her ex wouldn't be a *complete* asshole, but he'd proven his asshole tendencies were strong and that hope had been shattered anyway.

Later, when things became clear, she wouldn't be able to believe she hadn't recognized the stranger bearing sand toys at her front door.

But, in that moment, her mind wasn't anywhere close to sharp. In fact, she felt a bit like an elephant wearing rollerblades —big clumsy feet moving out of control in all directions, flailing and trying not to fall . . . even though the collapse was inevitable in the end.

And *that* was an image for the middle of the day.

Enough.

Her lawyer was doing what he could. She'd checked in with Alberto just that morning and he was filing . . . whatever lawyers filed with the court. So, she was focusing on her work. Her lesson plans were almost complete, her classroom supplies had been ordered. The first day of school loomed heavy with anticipation . . . and she might not be able to stay in this house.

Memories refused to be compartmentalized away.

This was the house she'd spent hour upon hour setting the tile backsplash in the kitchen, watching copious YouTube videos, fucking up so much, but still managing to make it look nearly perfect in the end—if one ignored the tile with spacing that was off in the corner by the fridge.

Which most people—most people being *not* her—did.

This house to which she'd brought Rylie home.

This house with the ocean, with waves, never failed to soothe her, with salt-tinged and sticky air that clung to her skin, mussed her hair.

This house where Rylie was asleep, cuddled up with her fox on their deck, those waves in the background, her book forgotten as they coaxed her into a nap.

God, *this* house. She loved it so much.

And yet, it was nothing when compared to the love she had for her little girl.

Shannon sighed, stepped out onto the deck, and made her way over to her daughter, scooping Ry up into her arms—albeit with a grunt, since at almost seven, Ry was getting to be a big kid and it wasn't an effortless lift any longer. More gym time was necessary, she supposed, as she carried her daughter inside.

She stepped over the threshold and stifled a giggle, thinking of what Pepper had told her the last time she'd lamented about needing more time for exercise.

"One, lifting your wine glass to your lips is exercise," the sweet redhead with a naughty streak had told her. Then had

gone on, proving that naughty streak by adding, *"Two, the best exercise is finding a hot guy and working your way through a pair of sheets."*

"Through?" Shannon had asked.

Pale skin flushed bright red, because even though Pepper had that dirty mind, her blush powers were strong. *"Through,"* she'd said. *"Improbable, unless you're me, who catches a heel and manages to tear my lovely, expensive thousand-thread-count sheets I argued with my husband over buying."*

"Who wanted them?"

A grin. *"Neither of us . . . and both of us."*

"Um, what?"

"Part of the fun with Derek is the debate."

Shannon had been married for years, but she had no clue what Pepper was talking about. *"What do you mean?"*

Green eyes on hers. *"I guess, I'm saying that even if we're bickering or arguing over stupidly expensive sheets"*—Pepper's face had softened—*"I know at the end of it, he loves me . . . and making up is half the battle."*

She didn't know what expression had crossed her face at Pepper's words, but her friend had paled, apologies beginning to drop from her lips.

Which was the point when Shan had shepherded her to the door.

Because she'd seen what was in Pepper's eyes.

And it was pity.

But no more pity than she felt for herself. She'd been with Brian since high school, and in all their years together, she'd never found what Pepper had.

No fighting and making up in bed.

No arguing about the small stuff because the big things were going wonderfully.

No . . . weighted looks only Derek and Pepper understood,

no inside jokes, no closeness or partnership or loving eyes.

Because she and Brian weren't meant to be.

Because Brian had fucked everything in sight.

Because . . . she'd let herself be in a relationship with a man who didn't see her value and instead of leaving, she'd been too afraid to be alone.

She set Rylie on the bed, tugging a light blanket over her and her stuffed fox, aptly named Foxy, but when she turned to the door, Shannon found her legs wouldn't carry her through it. Instead, she found herself moving to the rocking chair perched in one corner and sitting down.

How many hours had she sat there rocking Rylie?

How many hours had she sat there wishing that things were different?

Too many, she knew.

"Too many," she vowed because as she stared out the window, watching the waves, so beyond done with feeling this way. No. More. Shannon made a promise to herself, to her daughter. No more wishes. No more making herself small.

She was going to live.

She was going to fight.

And in doing so, she was going to give Rylie something *she* never had.

Herself.

A girl, a woman who didn't need reassurance from the outside world, or from a man, a partner, or even from her family, her friends. Ryle would have confidence inside and not look for it to be reinforced elsewhere.

But in order to do that, Shannon knew she needed to find it for herself first.

"I will, baby," she said, glancing over at the sleeping form of her daughter. "I promise. I'll fight for this. I'll fight for you. I'll fight for myself."

SIX

BEARING MORE THAN GIFTS

Finn

HE WAS KNOCKING on Shannon's door again.

But this time instead of returning lost toys, he came bearing gifts.

In the form of a giant fruit basket sent from his agent. One that was going to rot on his kitchen counter, because how in the fuck was he going to eat ten pounds of apples and oranges all on his own?

A freckled nose appeared in the window. "Mom! It's Mr. Finn."

He grinned and waved. "Hi, Rylie."

"Hi!" She waved back.

Then her face disappeared, and Shannon was there, dark circles under her eyes, recognition still not anywhere in the vicinity of her expression, but determination seemed to be present. "Hi, Mr. Finn." A quirk of her lips, amusing herself by echoing her daughter. Then the door cracked, and she leaned against the opening. "Everything okay?"

"Yeah. Also, you can just call me Finn."

"I don't know. Mr. Finn does have a certain ring to it," she teased.

"If you say so." He grinned and held up the basket. "I wanted to see if you and Rylie would take some fruit off my hands."

Her brows drew together.

"My ag—uh . . . *friend* sent me this, and it's way too much for one person to eat before it goes bad." He shrugged. "I just thought that most kids seem to like apples and oranges." A beat. "Or, at least, my nieces and nephews do."

"I *love* apples," Rylie said, skipping in. "Can I have one?" He nodded, and she glanced at her mother, who nodded as well, before scooping a shining red fruit from the basket he held. "Can I read on the deck, Mom?" she asked, lifting the apple to her lips.

"Wash it first," Shannon admonished. "And, yes, but what did you forget?"

Blue eyes streaked with brown met his, and Finn experienced another gut punch courtesy of the females in this house. Because where Shannon's eyes were tinged with sadness, Rylie's were bright and clear and startlingly happy.

"Thanks, Mr. Finn," Rylie said.

"You're welcome, Ms. Rylie."

A smile, a vivid burst of happiness before she sprinted off to the kitchen, where the water turned on for all of one second as she washed the fruit. Then footsteps raced across the hardwood, her, "excuse me," rushed but still there when she slipped by them to pass through the door. And then she was skidding to a stop in front of a chair on the deck, covering herself and her stuffed fox with a blanket before she pulled out a book.

The actions told him that she must have done the same routine time and again until it was second-nature, until she didn't think, just *knew* that was a place she could be safe and cuddle up with a book.

And his heart, the organ he'd thought numb and unfeeling, pulsed again.

"Um . . . did you want to come in for something to drink?" Shannon asked, stepping back.

Considering he was still standing on the threshold, a dozen apples and oranges—minus one—in his hands, that seemed like a good idea.

"Oh, can you leave that open?" she said, when he moved inside, started to close the door behind him. "I can't see Ry unless it is."

"Of course."

He spied a tiny doorstop in the shape of a starfish and used his foot to prop the wooden panel open then followed Shannon into the living room. It was smallish, like his, but the large front windows opened the space up. That along with the white couch, the gray and aquamarine accents, gave the room a calming, luxurious feel, and Finn knew the decorators he'd paid a boatload of money to decorate his house back in L.A. couldn't have done a better job.

In fact, if there hadn't been family pictures on the mantle, he could have believed it was the staged beach house in Malibu he'd been touring to buy before he'd hightailed it out of town.

He frowned.

"You okay?"

"No kid clutter."

"What?"

She had a rambunctious six-or-seven-year-old. A white couch with no stains on it, no Legos littering the pale gray carpet, no rogue banana peels or juice boxes or—

"What are you staring at?"

He jumped and spun toward Shannon, seeing she was

watching him carefully. While he'd been staring off into space like a dumbass. Cool. "Who designed this for you?"

"What do you mean?" she asked, frowning. "I did."

"No. Who picked out the furniture?" Finn turned in a circle. "Who did the placement? The color scheme?"

Her frown went deeper. "I did."

"But you have a kid," he said, coming toward her and setting the basket on the glass coffee table—yes, a glass coffee table. "How is it that the couch doesn't have stains? How is it that there aren't toys scattered everywhere?"

Shannon's face relaxed, her mouth twitching up at the corners. "Rylie *is* pretty good at cleaning up after herself— though I've all but given up with her room. After spending many hours organizing and then *re*-organizing her toys, both with and without her, I now abide by the *there's a door, so close it, and move on* mentality."

He snorted, remembering the chaos in his home, being one of five kids who ran wild, and as his mom frequently stated, giving her a multitude of gray hairs. "I think that was the only way my mom made it through our childhood."

She chuckled. "Well, I'm definitely glad I'm not alone."

"No, you're not."

Shannon froze. Probably because his words were soft, and his tone sounded real crazy. Repeat, *real* crazy. Quiet and husky, as though they were lovers sharing a moment, and not virtual strangers.

"Um . . ." She bit her lip.

He cleared his throat, pushed down the desire. For God's sake, he was an actor. He'd pretended his whole life. He pretended for a living. This—making light conversation with a beautiful woman—should be easy.

"That is, you have Rylie," he said, thankfully pulling something semi-normal out of nowhere. "Your daughter is great."

Shannon's face softened. "She is." A beat, lips curving. "Also, it should be noted that the person who's made the biggest mess on this couch is me, drinking—or well, *spilling*, a glass of red wine"—she rolled her eyes at herself—"luckily for me, the covers come off, and everything is machine washable."

"Smart."

Her lips curved up fully, and she shrugged. "Occasionally."

"I think," he said, considering the warm and cozy house, the lovely little kid on the porch, the self-effacing humor and the solid parenting, "a lot more than occasionally."

She stared at him for a beat. "Thanks," she whispered, then, "Please, sit," she added, sinking down onto the couch.

And immediately popped to her feet on a wince.

Finn opened his mouth to ask if she was okay, but then she moved a pillow and held up a plastic unicorn with a seriously deadly-looking horn. "What were you saying about not seeing toys scattered everywhere?"

He snorted. "To Rylie's credit, it appears to be less scattered and more strategically placed."

She laughed.

His breath caught, heart squeezing at the lovely, light sound, one that seemed to fit so well in this room and yet one that he had the feeling was rare.

Because even during the conversation, even though she was bantering with him, the hurt was still there. Beneath the surface, calling his white knight tendencies to high alert, even though he had a boatload of his own problems and had absolutely no business even considering playing the white knight.

But also . . . this woman didn't need a white knight.

Just as he could feel the sadness, he could sense that much as well.

She might be hurt, but she was also strong. Fragile exterior, steel beneath.

And that push-pull made her the most interesting person he'd met in a long time.

"I really am impressed by the space you created," he said into the quiet that had fallen, taking a seat next to her when she lowered herself back onto the couch.

Shannon frowned. "You're not a real estate agent, are you?"

"What? No," he said. "I just . . . studied design for a bit." Which was true, if someone considered a *bit* being three weeks in preparation for a movie role where he played a designer whose life was falling apart.

Maybe he should have studied the life falling apart portion of the story more than fleshing out his design skills.

"Sometimes good window dressings make all the difference."

"That and closed doors," he quipped.

"True." Her lips quirked. Her eyes warmed.

"Can I offer you something to drink?" she asked, gesturing toward a doorway that led through to the kitchen, if the glimpse of white cabinets Finn could see was any indication.

"Got anything that goes well with apples?"

There.

Every nerve in his body stood at attention.

Because *there* it was. Finally.

And her smile—a real one—was just as incredible as he'd thought it would be. It was almost tangible, caressing his skin, warming him from the inside out, making his lips tingle with need, his cock twitch.

All from a smile.

Inner alarm bells rang out, signaling danger.

But it was danger he didn't want to avoid. It was danger he *wanted*. A slippery slope that was both intoxicating and terrifying.

"Come into the kitchen, Finn," she said, pushing to her feet. "And I'll rock your world."

"Why does that sound like a challenge?" He lifted a brow.

"Have you ever had peanut butter milk and apples?"

"Can't say I have." He made a face. "Also, I can't say that peanut butter milk sounds good."

"Okay, honey." The real smile never left her face, her soft words drifting down Finn's spine. "You come into my kitchen, and I'll rock your world."

His breath caught and he followed her into the other room, ready to be rocked

But the truth was that she'd already rocked his world.

With her smile and her sad eyes. With her laughter and poking fun at herself. With how she looked at and talked to her daughter. Even before he tried her peanut butter milk—which was really more milkshake than milk and delicious as hell.

It should also be noted *that* rocked his world as well.

SEVEN

NO TEARS SPILLED, ONLY MILK

Shannon

SHE HURRIED TO THE KITCHEN, cheeks blazing.

Honey.

Why in the devil had she called him *honey?*

Because he was gorgeous, because she used the word *honey* a lot with her students, with Rylie, with—

Because his eyes were the color of honey.

Dripping, golden honey, warmed and readied to be poured over hot oatmeal or dribbled into her tea, or—

Those eyes were on hers, questions in their depths.

Shan got moving. Peanut butter, cups, and the blender from the cabinets, milk from the fridge. Realizing she'd left the apples on the table, she moved to get them, but Finn asked, "Where are you going?"

She froze. "Um . . . we need apples to have peanut butter milk and apples."

"I'll get them."

"Oh—" A shake of her head. "You don't have to. I can—"

He left the room.

Shannon's mouth fell open, trying to remember when Brian had ever offered to get something for her, much less had actually gone to get it when she said he didn't have to.

And, damn.

Brian invading her thoughts again.

She was really fucking tired of that.

Pretty hard for her ex to *not* be doing that. Especially when she'd spoken with her lawyer that morning and had heard her only course of action was to contest the divorce and hope a judge would allow her to do it so late in the process.

Almost done with Brian . . . and then pulled right back in.

Now, wasn't that the story of her life?

Finn walked back in on the heels of that thought, basket in his hands, gorgeous face open and relaxed. And yet, she had the notion that it was a mask, that his inside was as messed up as hers.

Twisted, knotted, damaged . . .

And she was just standing there again.

Finn grabbed three apples from the basket, not two, and warmth filled her. Without a word or prompt, this man had thought of her daughter.

A curl of cynicism wove through her, quickly chasing away that warmth.

Hell, he was a big guy. He was probably planning on eating two apples himself. But just as she was going down the dark spiral of cursing all men on Earth, Finn held up one shining red fruit. "Will Rylie be too full for another apple?" A beat. "Or have tummy trouble?"

Cynicism disappeared.

Hope bubbled. Okay, maybe there was more than one good guy in the world (that *one* good guy being, Derek, Pepper's husband, of course), because this man, quite literally bearing fruit, remembering that her daughter would want a snack, too, being nice and funny, even though she was just a neighbor, was displaying serious good guy street cred. Well, that and using a phrase like *tummy trouble.*

Her lips tipped up. "Tummy trouble?"

A shrug, but his profile gave her a glimpse of a slightly-reddened swathe of cheek, one stripe of pink skin topping the dark brown stubble adorning his jaw. "My sister has reinforced in me the danger of too much fruit."

"Why does there seem to be more to that story?"

More red.

But less talking.

"Finn." Her teacher voice came out unintentionally, something that Brian had always hated, something she didn't use on purpose, but also . . . something that just happened sometimes.

Instead of getting mad, however—like Brian would have done—Finn turned enough to meet her stare. "That tone is dangerous," he teased. "Threatens to make a man want to give up *all* of his secrets."

Her breath caught as she wondered what kind of secrets this gorgeous man might have, but just as she was mentally paging through the possibilities of him being a secret agent or a professional surfer or an Italian chef, he asked, "Can you tell me where your knives and cutting boards are?"

Surfer. With tanned skin like that, he was either a surfer or an Italian chef, but he was here in Stoneybrooke. In a cottage on the beach. So, surfing.

Definitely that.

Though an Italian chef, one who specialized in all types of pasta, would be awesome.

Also . . . special agent was still a possibility, especially with those secrets in his gaze.

"Shannon?"

"Hmm?" she murmured, lost in the image of him prowling

down the street, taking out bad guys left and right. What? Yes, she knew it was unrealistic. No, the idea of him handcuffing her, pinning her against the wall, or better yet on a bed was a bad one. But still tempting—

She shook her head, snapping herself out of it.

Though, maybe she was finally snapping out of it, of how she'd been with Brian, of how she'd shrunk into herself, trying not to feel *anything*, including desire, in an effort to not be hurt again.

Because desire was a big feel.

And that made her think that finally, a year after finding out about the lies and deceptions, that someday she might be whole—

No, that someday she might be *more*.

Yeah, more. More than just a woman with a man. But a person, fully-formed with ideas and thoughts and not a wilting flower who shrank herself down, just to fit.

And . . . she liked that. A lot.

Another promise to herself, to her daughter. Keep growing. Keep strengthening.

"Cutting board and knife?"

She blinked. "What?"

"Do you have a cutting board and knife?"

"Why?" she asked, brows drawing down.

"To cut"—his honey eyes danced with amusement—"the apples."

"Why?" she repeated, totally flummoxed. Was he seriously offering to help her cook? Or cut, rather?

He tilted his head to the side. "Does your fancy peanut butter milk and apples recipe have a special way of slicing the apples?"

She shook her head. "No."

"So"—his mouth twitched—"I'll cut them."

"But—"

"Cutting board?"

She took a step toward the cabinet that held her cutting boards. "Here, I'll—"

"No, Blue Eyes," he said, putting his hand on her arm. "Just point. I can get it myself."

She bit the inside of her lip, a thrill skirting through her. *More.* Yes, maybe she could be more than she'd ever hoped.

But she had to actually speak and talk like a live human being.

Or, well . . . point anyway.

She indicated the cabinet.

He grinned, opened the door, rustled around inside, and extracted a wooden cutting board. Which gave this man, this neighbor she barely knew, extra points. Because he knew without her telling him that plastic was for meat and wood was for fruits and vegetables.

"Knife?" he asked.

She pointed again.

Another grin as he opened the drawer, grabbed out a chef's knife, then reached for the towel she kept by the sink, folded and tucked it underneath the cutting board— ensuring the wood wouldn't slip on the counter as he was using it. Then he picked up the three apples and carried them to the sink. "I'm guessing you're used to supervising in the kitchen."

"Um, yes?"

He turned on the water.

"I promise I can cut three apples."

Now, *her* cheeks went hot, but she just nodded, turned to the cabinet in front of her and snagged three glasses—two glass, one plastic, because as Finn had noted, Rylie would definitely want in on this.

Milk into the blender. Three heaping spoons full of peanut butter.

Flick the switch.

And thick, creamy, frothy peanut butter milk was born.

Also, yes, she was well-aware of what kind of images thick, creamy, and frothy conjured up, but she also didn't care because her peanut butter milk was that delicious. Add in dipping slices of fresh and juicy—*ha!*—apples, and it was the best snack on the planet.

Ry had appeared in the kitchen by the time the blender switched off, her eyes wide as she bounced on her toes.

"Peanut butter milk?" she exclaimed, still bouncing as her gaze flicked to Finn. "And apples?"

"Mmm-hmm," she said, pouring the milk into the three glasses.

"My favorite!" Ry danced her way over.

Shan pressed a kiss to her head. "Want to carefully take these out to the table on the deck?"

"Okay!" She grabbed two of the glasses and made her way carefully outside.

Smiling at the dainty steps her normally bull-in-a-china-shop daughter took as she was careful to not spill a single drop of nirvana, Shan watched her head out the front door, then turned and grabbed three small plates, setting them in front of Finn.

Who was deliberately cutting the apples into the most perfect slices she had ever seen.

Evenly cut. Not a trace of a core in sight. Skin removed and piled neatly in one corner of the board.

Italian chef.

Tall, dark, and with killer knife skills . . . yeah, that would still do well for her fantasies. Though, really, Shannon couldn't argue that she could, just as easily, picture this man as a firefighter or a politician or that secret agent, who'd shown up looking uncertain on her porch with sand toys a few days ago, with fruit today and had commented on the placement of her furniture then had made himself comfortable in her kitchen before efficiently slicing fruit.

Different faces.

Yet, this man wasn't lost in them. His essence never seemed to fully leave.

So, a chameleon, but not deceiver—not like Brian.

He was just . . . a crystal turning over in her palm, the sun hitting different angles, reflecting the light in constantly changing ways—rainbows and white light, shadows and the sun seeping through into her skin—but still, intrinsically, that crystal in her palm. This man in front of her was exactly that.

Revealing different layers, showing off different facets.

Layers. Onions have layers.

She smiled, thinking of the quote from Rylie's favorite movie about a green ogre who found his heart.

"What is it?"

A soft question that made her realize she'd been staring at him, pondering too heavily to realize he'd filled the plates with apples, that he'd turned to face her.

Now, more cheek heating—on her part.

Because she *had* been staring . . . and because for the first time, in a long time, she was studying a man and finding him not only beautiful and desirous but also fascinating.

This wasn't a sexy A-list celebrity on a magazine cover she was appreciating at a distance. Or Pepper's Derek who was gorgeous, but not hers, so there wasn't room there for desire—wouldn't *ever* be room there. This wasn't even Brian, who she'd once wanted so badly, the hormones of teenagedom intense and overwhelming.

This was . . . peeling off *her* layers of hurt.

This was *her* realizing clearly that just because she wanted Rylie's life to be different, to be more, that just because she would fight tooth and nail for her daughter to have a full life, that it also didn't mean Shannon's couldn't be different and more, too.

Fingers on her cheek made her jump.

But not pull back.

They *should* have. This contact from Finn, who she'd barely spent any time with.

Except, it didn't feel wrong. Rather, it felt as though that touch, the soft brush of roughened fingers on her skin was a lightning rod, cracking through the numb, the fog of pain and betrayal, arrowing straight for her center and making her *feel*.

And *God* did she feel.

"Shannon?" he asked, concern on his face.

"Shrek," she blurted.

Finn's head tilted to the side. "Shrek?"

A nod. "I'm Shrek. I just—" She shrugged. "I just . . . I'm *Shrek*."

"The ogre?"

She nodded again.

His brows drew together. "I—"

She was so distracted by their conversation—well, by her thinking and random blurting—that Rylie had slipped in undetected.

At least, until she heard the crash.

As one, they turned, saw Ry standing in the kitchen, the last cup of milk having slipped from her hands and hitting the floor. Of course, it was a glass one, and now her daughter was standing over a growing puddle littered with shards.

"Oh, honey," she groaned, unable to stop herself.

And, as one would predict, that was the exact wrong thing to say when a kid made a mistake and clearly felt bad about it.

She knew that.

She'd gone to school and learned techniques to avoid just this exact reaction.

Which was Rylie's face crumpling, tears pouring down her face.

"I-I didn't mean to—"

Shan opened her mouth to reassure Ry that, of course, she didn't mean to, but Finn had already moved, scooping Rylie up from the puddle and away from the sharp pieces of glass.

"Of course, you didn't," he said. "It was an accident." He set her on the counter, eyeing her bare feet carefully before extracting the towel from beneath his cutting board and gently wiping the soles. "Did you get cut?" he asked.

Rylie shook her head, eyes drifting down over Finn's shoulder. "I'm sorry, Mommy."

Shannon had moved to pick up the broken glass and was dumping it into the trash. She shut the cabinet, stepped over the puddle, and moved to her daughter. "Oh, baby. It's okay. It was just an accident."

Ry sniffed.

"Come here." Shan tugged her in for a hug. "There's no crying over spilled milk," she said, pulling back and wiping Rylie's eyes.

"Yes, there is," her daughter replied, calm now, her eyes slightly reddened.

Shannon laughed but caught Ry when she started to climb down from the counter. "Hang on, baby," she said. "Let me clean up the milk—"

"It's done."

She turned, saw Finn throwing away a wad of dirty paper towels, her bottle of kitchen cleaner in his hands.

"I should sweep."

He picked up the dustpan he must have pulled from

beneath the sink, sweeping quickly and efficiently as her mouth dropped open.

"I—"

"Why don't you carry Rylie outside?"

"But one of us won't have milk!" Ry's bottom lip wobbled. "Because I dropped it."

"Honey."

Finn stood. "I don't need milk."

"But it's Mommy's special drink, and you should have some." That lip was pushed out into a pout.

"Ry—"

He opened the cabinet with her glasses and pulled out one. "Why don't you and your mom pour some from your glasses in this one? That way, we can all share."

Her daughter smiled and grabbed the cup, holding it close to her chest. "Okay!"

Shannon lifted her off the counter and safely out of the way, setting her on her feet just outside the kitchen. "Finn—"

Honey eyes came to hers.

"Go, sweetheart," he murmured. "I can do this."

She nodded, turned to follow Ry, but then she turned back. "Finn—"

"Let me help you, dammit," he gritted, not sharp, but rough and frustrated and punctuated by a sigh. "I can sweep one floor."

She bit back a smile, somehow charmed by the big, smart, pushy, sweet man whom she'd pushed to grumpiness. "I was just going to say that the vacuum is in the hall closet."

"Oh." He bent, started sweeping the floor again.

"Finn?"

A beat then, "Yeah?" Still not sharp. Still gruff.

Still making her smile.

"Thanks."

"You're welcome, sweetheart."

Yeah, still gruff.

Yeah, she liked it.

A lot.

So much that her cheeks hurt when she walked out to join Rylie on the deck, and for the first time in many years, it was because she was happy and touched and not because she was holding back tears.

EIGHT
ALL THE BAKED GOODS

Finn

HE HAD to admit that peanut butter milk was the shit.

The apples were . . . well, apples.

But Shannon had been right. Together it was pretty much the perfect snack. Though, Finn knew that was mostly because of the two females sitting next to him. One, rather, since the soon-to-be-seven-year-old Rylie was now perfecting her sand-castle skills on the beach in front of them.

And he was left with a full belly, warm sunshine on his skin, and this woman next to him, silently watching the waves.

Then she turned her eyes, so similar to the color of the ocean, onto him.

Arrested.

His body. His breath.

That gaze pinned him in place more intensely than the hard-ass director who'd given him his big break.

"Why are you here?"

How to answer that?

Did he give the canned answer? Exhaustion. Working too

hard for too many years and he just needed some time to himself?

Or did he tell this woman, this virtual stranger, the beautiful sad female who he was somehow connected with, the dark secret that had been eating at him. The reason he'd flipped out on camera. The reason he'd been sent away, and not just by his agent and publicist.

But by his family.

To get the paparazzi away.

Because Finn hadn't just lost it on camera. He had a meltdown on a live morning TV show, calling out the anchor for something he'd seen backstage—the anchor cornering a young, female intern—thus triggering a media shitstorm, but also the coming forward of victims of that anchor, and a subsequent firing. He'd been lauded—bravo for stepping up!—and reviled—just another male wanting to be a savior when the system was broken—and he'd deserved both actions in equal measures. Especially because his actions and words hadn't been truly altruistic. He'd seen that girl, young and innocent and her fire and hope dying in her as the anchor had slid his hand over her ass . . . and he had just been so tired of it all, so fucking tired of the duplicity of Hollywood calling for equality and kindness when he saw this same type of mistreatment, time and *time* again.

Witnessing the assault had been shit timing.

He'd seen it just after he'd found out about his sister the weekend before.

And where he would have normally taken care, treaded carefully, and not thrown the victim's story straight into the gobbling jaws of the media and its circus, Finn hadn't been thinking straight.

So . . . he'd snapped.

He'd remembered all the times someone young and vulnerable had been taken advantage of and he hadn't been able to do anything because he'd heard about it afterward. All the times he'd been there and failed to intervene when he should have.

Crude jokes.

A laughing innuendo that wasn't shared all around.

And his sister.

His baby sister.

The timing of those two things . . . and he'd lost it.

"My younger sister was raped," he said quietly.

Shannon's startled inhale told him everything he needed to know. "Oh no," she murmured. "I'm so sorry that happened to her."

"Me, too."

She nodded, eyes drifting back to the waves. "But"—he held his breath as the rest of her words came—"that doesn't explain why you're here," she finished softly.

His breath slid out. "No," he murmured. "It doesn't."

Gaze on the horizon, she waited, not pushing for an explanation, not demanding he tell her more. Just sitting quietly and patiently, and Finn found that for the first time in a long time, the words just came.

Not a struggle.

Not painful.

Just as easy as breathing.

Thus was the power of Shannon, he supposed. This woman, whom he'd been connected to since returning the pink plastic bucket, a thread extending from him to her as he'd handed it over, looping back around.

And so, he found he could tell her, "She wanted me to go."

A beat. A soft creak as she shifted in her chair, facing him. Still not speaking, but her expression open and willing to listen.

"I freaked out." He shook his head. "I absolutely lost it. I wanted to destroy every single male on the planet, myself included. We created this fucked-up world that allows women to be hurt and . . ."

"And it was your baby sister."

It was that. Exactly that. The little sister he'd helped up when she'd fallen while learning to ride a bike. The one who punched out her asshole of a high school boyfriend when he broke up with her the day before prom and then took her best friend to the dance. He'd learned to braid her hair when his older sister Kathy had gone off to college.

"Lexie has the biggest heart of anyone I know."

"She was hurt in an impossible way." Shannon released a slow breath. "And you couldn't protect her."

He nodded. "Yes," he said. "Then I upset her more."

By exposing her to the media. By having a meltdown that was documented everywhere. By making a painful moment even more agonizing.

Shannon went quiet again, but eventually she asked softly, "Are you sure she wanted you to leave?"

"The words *Finn, you need to go*, made it pretty clear."

"I'm sorry." Her hand found his, squeezed lightly. "I don't think that anyone can ever know the proper way to react in situations like that. It's such a visceral, hurtful thing, a-and my heart breaks for her."

His chin dropped to his chest. "Thanks for saying that," he murmured. "I'm sorry to be a damper on our afternoon."

Startling blue eyes on his, warm and soft. "Not at all. I needed the reminder."

He frowned.

She shook her head. "Sorry, I didn't mean that like it sounded. I just . . . I've had a rough time of it lately, and I needed the kick in the ass to remember that my hurts aren't any bigger than anyone else's."

He flipped his hand over, laced his fingers through hers. "That's not what I was trying—"

"I know, honey." A smile.

Different this time. Not sad, but not filled with amusement either. It was warm, soft, and it melted something inside him.

Fuck he liked this woman.

"My husband—"

The blood in his veins froze.

"—well, my soon-to-be-ex-husband, has been cheating on me." The breath released, relief that she wasn't married, or well, this wasn't what he'd imagined for a split second. That relief warred with sympathy because he'd been on the receiving end of cheating more than once, and it sucked.

"I'm sorry."

She made a noise of disgust. "Me, too. Even more to find out that he'd been cheating since almost our wedding day and that he has another family . . . with a little boy about Rylie's age."

"Fuck."

He hadn't meant to say that aloud, not with little ears around. But then again, neither of their stories had been meant for little ears.

A ghost of a smile. "You don't have to look so chagrined," she teased. "I *have* heard that word before."

He chuckled. "My sister, Kathy. The older one with kids," he added, though she probably didn't need the extra details of his life. Not after all he'd bombarded her with. "She's trained me well."

"We moms are good at that."

"It's true."

"And," she went on, "just to get it all out there. I let him have everything—the funds in our joint bank accounts, my right to his retirement, refused alimony and child support—on the condition that he would let Rylie and me have the house."

Finn's stomach twisted.

Because he had the feeling that this story wasn't going to end with a surprise, *Then my ex let me have the house AND half of everything else.*

Unfortunately, he was right.

Shannon's expression hardened. "Then last week, he sent a real estate agent to the house."

"To look?"

"To sell," she said. "Because it's in his name, not mine." Then she explained about the bed rest and hospital stay, the complications after Rylie's delivery and how she'd been out of it when her ex had done all the papers.

"But it's community property," Finn said. "If it's acquired during the marriage, shouldn't it be part of the settlement?" A shake of his head. "Aren't you entitled to fifty percent—"

She nodded. "Of the profits."

"He wants his half."

"I don't think Brian knows what he wants," she said softly. "But I do know that he's not going to abide by our agreement."

"Shit. I'm sorry."

A shrug. "My lawyer is doing his best."

"I can—"

He'd started to offer up his lawyers, his resources, but then Rylie appeared in a skid of sand and bare feet. "Mom! Come see!"

Shannon pushed out of the chair, her hand slipping free from his.

Finn missed the contact almost immediately.

But then he realized it was a good thing Ry had interrupted him. The last time he'd gotten involved, pushed his way into a situation that didn't involve him, it had blown up in his and Lexie's faces.

He didn't want that for Shannon.

And him siccing his lawyers on this asshole ex of Shannon's was sure to get the vultures circling.

Descending.

He watched her smiling as she ooh-ed and ahh-ed over the sandcastle, and he knew that he couldn't do that to her. So, instead of offering her the power of his name and his retinue of lawyers, Finn carried the dirty glasses and plates into the kitchen, washing and loading them in the dishwasher as his mom had trained him to do many moons before.

Then he slipped quietly from the deck and vowed to leave this woman to her life.

His vow LASTED all of twelve hours.

Which was how long it took for the knock to come on his door.

He was reading over a script. Well, reading was a strong word for slogging his way through another uninspired story. Sighing as he set it back onto the pile of scripts his agent had sent over, Finn pushed to his feet and headed for the door.

A freckled nose, blue-brown eyes, and a rapid wave.

He smiled and cracked the door. "Morning, Rylie."

"Mornin'!" She shoved a foil-wrapped loaf into his hands. "Mom said we could share."

He took the parcel instinctively. "Th—"

"Bye!"

She ran off, meeting a redheaded female wearing a large floppy hat and a big grin. The woman bent and high-fived Rylie then straightened as she handed her another loaf, presumably to deliver to the next lucky neighbor.

But as she was straightening, she froze in a half-bent position.

"Finn?" She popped up like a whack-a-mole, recognition collecting on her face.

For one heartbeat, his stomach seized, dread at being recognized coalescing in a nearly impossible to resist urge to run into the house and slam the door closed. In fact, he'd actually taken a step back when the bright red hair, the porcelain skin, the—as she tripped over her own feet—charming clumsiness processed.

"Pepper?" he asked.

She nodded, sweeping toward him and tugging him in for a hug.

Well, less hugging and more catching her as she tripped again, but the end result was his old friend in his arms, smiling and . . . happy.

She seemed *really* happy.

"Married life agrees with you," he said, releasing her, his eyes drifting over her shoulder to make sure that Rylie hadn't wandered off.

When he saw Ry, he grinned.

"Oh," Pepper said, turning. "Ry is good about not running —" She broke off on a laugh.

Because Rylie had plunked down onto the sand, unwrapped the final foil loaf, and was eating it like it was the last food on earth.

"She's something else," he murmured.

"Oh, have you met Rylie already?" she asked, lacing her arm through his. "And Shannon? How long have you been in town? How long are you staying?" Emerald eyes flicked up to his. "You're the one person I like from the old crew, and you didn't let me know you were coming?"

He waited.

She huffed. "Are you going to answer me?"

"I was just waiting to see if you were done lobbing questions at me," he teased. "You sure you don't want back into the industry? You would be an excellent investigative interviewer."

"Ha." Pepper snorted. "I'd be more likely to trip them into question submission."

"Don't you know that clumsy heroines are in style?" he asked, tugging the end of her ponytail.

A shudder. "I've had more than enough clumsy for a lifetime. I don't need to trade in it."

"You're okay, though?" He tugged her to a stop. "Happy with this guy and your art? Happy being away from L.A.?"

"Happier than I ever thought possible."

His heart squeezed. "I'm so glad to hear that."

They reached Rylie on the heels of his statement, the little girl's bare feet covered in sand, the loaf of banana bread—if it was the same deliciousness he could smell wafting up from the loaf in his hand—open as she broke off chunks and crammed them into her mouth.

"Rylie!" Pepper exclaimed.

The little girl looked up guiltily. "Sorry?" she said, the word barely distinguishable around the bite in her mouth.

"I guess the Hamiltons aren't getting their loaf," Pepper said.

"Nope," he agreed. "It doesn't look that way."

"Want some?" Rylie asked, holding up the bread.

"No, thanks," he and Pepper said in unison.

Rylie went back to eating.

"Are you going to answer any of my questions?" Pepper asked again.

"I've been in town a week."

Her head tilted to the side. "Why are you saying that like there's something else I should know?"

Finn's jaw dropped open, gaze dropping to the sand and Rylie then back up to Pepper's face, which was clouded with concern but didn't have a trace of recognition. "Do you really not know?"

Concern transmuted to worry. "What happened?"

His eyes flicked to Ry. "Lexie. Me. The media."

She couldn't possibly ferret everything out from those three words, but Pepper had been part of a long Hollywood dynasty, and that gave her enough.

"So you're here?"

"For exhaustion," he quipped.

Her nose wrinkled. "Shi—er, *shoot*, Finn."

He shrugged. "It'll pass."

"Yeah," she said. "That's true. It'll pass, and in the meantime, you get this"—she swung a hand toward the ocean—"waves and privacy. No one in this town cares about movies or the latest gossip." She nodded toward Ry. "They care about good schools and who has the best recipe for banana bread. Shannon's is the best," she added with a smile. "Just in case you were wondering."

"I was definitely wondering that," he deadpanned.

She rolled her eyes. "Punk."

"I'm glad to see you, Red."

"Me, too. We should have dinner—" Movement to their side caught both of their attention. "Oh, and maybe Shannon could join, too. Have you met . . .?"

Her words trailed off.

Probably because he'd lost the ability to focus on them. Perhaps she'd stopped talking altogether because she got a glimpse of his face—which had to be revealing something of the visceral gut punch of Shannon, striding across the sand in a simple, almost prim, sapphire one-piece that showcased every lithe curve in sharp relief.

So. Fucking. Pretty.

She had a towel under one arm, a big floppy hat on her head, and sunglasses covering those gorgeous eyes.

And quite simply, she took his breath away.

"Finn," she said with a smile.

"Shannon," he murmured.

A soft question. "Want to watch the waves with us?"

He nodded . . . because words wouldn't come.

"Great!" Then her eyes drifted to Rylie, and her mouth dropped open. "Ry! How *could* you?"

His gaze rose to Pepper's and they shared a wince, realizing they probably should have stopped Rylie from downing that loaf instead of spending the time catching up.

But the damage was done.

The loaf decimated.

And for the first time in a long time, Finn figured he might as well live for a minute. He bent, scooped a chunk of the bread out and shoved it into his mouth. "Whoops," he said, lips twitching as he chewed.

"Your bread is just too tempting," Pepper said, mirroring him.

Shannon plunked her hands on her hips, the towel falling to the sand. "Really?" she asked, scooping it up.

He shrugged and swallowed. "It really is too tempting."

He meant *she* was too tempting, and both Shannon and Pepper seemed to recognize that. Pepper gave him an assessing glance, but he was more focused on Shan and her lips parting, breath shuddering out.

Yeah.

Too fucking tempting.

Rylie stood and handed him the loaf. "Tempting!" she yelled and ran off.

He grinned as he traced her loping over the dunes, and he thought the little girl *was* tempting, albeit in a wholly different way than her mom. Sweet and fun and innocent, it was hard not to get swept up in her enthusiasm.

"I'll trade you," he told Pepper, carefully wrapping the half-eaten loaf while passing over his neatly wrapped one. "This can be for the Hamiltons."

"That's nice of you."

"You can take it to the Hamiltons," he said.

Yes, he emphasized *you* and *take*, even while understanding he probably didn't need to, given the knowing look Pepper tossed in his direction.

"You know the Hamiltons?" Shannon asked.

"No, Blue Eyes."

Shannon bit her lip. "But you'll take the half-eaten loaf anyway?"

"I've had my fingers inside it," he said, "that's a pretty sure-fire way to take ownership of the loaf."

She sucked in a breath.

Pepper made a strangled sound. "Well, I'll just go grab Ry and deliver this . . . unfingered loaf . . ."

He nodded but couldn't tear his eyes from Shannon to look at his old friend. No, his gaze was glued on the blue-eyed, pink-lipped, lithely curved woman in front of him, her skin bronzed by the morning sun, that prim and proper swimsuit making him want to peel it slowly from her body, kissing his way down and—

"You make excellent banana bread, Blue Eyes."

Another hitch in her breathing. "I—"

He waited to see if she'd finish the sentence, and when she didn't, he stepped closer. "You?" he asked softly.

Her body drifted toward his, her nipples beading against the fabric of the swimsuit, making his mouth ache, his skin prickle with the need to feel them pressed to his chest.

"Finn," she murmured.

Her mouth was *right* there.

"Shannon," he murmured back.

She rose on tiptoe, leaned in, and he bit back a groan when the pebbled buds of her nipples brushed his chest. He lifted his free hand slowly, threading it through the silken ends of her dark brown hair, tilting her head back, dropping his mouth toward hers.

Her lips were a millimeter away.

Hot breath. Sweet, floral scent.

"*Oh my God!* You're Finn Stoneman!"

NINE

PENGUIN SOCKS AND REALITY STRIKES

Shannon

SHE JERKED BACK, Finn's fingers getting tangled in her hair, the sharp but momentary pain the final push she needed to jump back into her own brain.

Physical and emotional.

She needed distance in both. Her eyes flicked to the side and saw a teenager standing a few feet away, her phone in hand, bobbing excitedly on her tiptoes. "Can I have a selfie?"

Finn stiffened, carefully slipped his hand free of Shannon's hair, then turned, but not before she saw a smile turn up the edges of his mouth.

A familiar smile.

A fucking smile that had graced billboards and magazine covers and . . . movie screens.

He knew Pepper.

He'd told her his real name. Finn. Stoneman.

But he wasn't referred to by both names. Or, at least, not often. He was just Finn, like Rhianna or Madonna or Beyonce, known by just one name. Four letters, one handsome face, one award-winning, charmingly self-effacing actor.

The actor.

He stepped toward the teenager, held the cell phone in a practiced way that illustrated quite clearly her realization was indeed the correct one.

God, how could she not have seen it before?

This man was quite possibly the most famous actor in the world.

Even Shannon, who didn't watch T.V., who had a soon-to-be-seven-year-old and so didn't go to the movies often, if at all, had seen this man.

She'd even felt there was something familiar about him.

But she hadn't clued in.

Fuck.

How could she have been so stupid?

"Thanks!" the teenager said happily. "I really loved you in *River Creek*. But my favorite is *Fled*."

"Thank you for saying that," Finn replied. "You're very kind."

Shannon wanted to sink down into the sand, for it to swallow her up and bury her. She'd been toe-to-toe with this man, this world-famous celebrity, and as the realization of how different their lives were . . . different? *Hell*. They were fucking universes away from one another.

The girl drifted away with one more smile, but Shan already knew what she needed to do.

That was to get the fuck out of there.

To focus on her own life.

To stop having moments of insanity, to stop pretending that she lived in a world where a brown girl could fall for a sexy, sweet white guy, who happened to be a huge movie star, and he fell for her right back.

Because that didn't happen.

That wasn't real life.

Not *her* life anyway.

She had to focus on Rylie. She wasn't even divorced yet. She—

Needed to go.

She spun, spotting Rylie returning from the Hamiltons', Pepper at her side as they made their way down to the water. Perfect. The ocean. She could dive in and drown herself. She high-tailed it that way.

"Shannon!" Finn called.

Nope. There was no way she was turning around. No way she could face this man whom she should have recognized instantly but was too much of a hot fucking mess to have done so.

The biggest movie star in the world was her neighbor.

And she'd made him peanut butter milk.

She groaned, dropped her eyes to the sand, and walked away like the speedy motherfucker she was.

"Shan."

Hot breath in her ear. A warm palm on her arm, slowing her, tugging her to a stop. "Wait, honey."

She shook her head even as she let him stall her feet, pull her to a halt.

"You really didn't recognize me?"

Shannon sighed. "No."

Silence then, "I know this is going to make me sound like an asshole," he said. "But . . . how?"

Her eyes were glued to the surf. "I-I'm busy."

"Busy?" he repeated.

"Yeah," she said. "And well, I used to be addicted to gossip shows, but then I met Pepper, and I realized how wrong and invasive they are . . . and things with Brian went to hell and . . . I just stopped watching."

"You've had a lot of other things to process."

She tugged her arm free. "I've got my head above water." A beat. "But most of the time it feels like I'm just barely above the surface. Still, I'm there. I'm not drowning."

Anymore.

No.

Not then. Not now. Not in the future.

"Enjoy the bread," she said. "And your time away from the press and—" Her lungs froze, the words stoppering up in the back of her throat, and she couldn't stop herself from spinning to face him again, to stare into those honey eyes she should have instantly recognized. "Your sister."

His lids closed, slid back open. "Yeah."

"And the media found out?"

"Because I told them." Her breath hitched, but he went on, explaining what he'd seen backstage, then about his on-screen meltdown, calling out the morning anchor, the situation with his sister slipping out in the process.

When he stopped talking, Shannon was at a loss for words.

What could she say aside from, "I'm so sorry."

He sighed. "The invasion of privacy is my burden for wanting to be in the industry. It's the nature of the business, and my family has never wanted the business, the connections, but they've put up with the negatives because they love me and want me to be happy."

"And you think you ruined that?"

Finn scoffed. "*Of course*, I ruined that. I was so furious that it happened to *my* sister, to someone in *my* family that I made it about me instead of recognizing that my sister needed me not to be angry, but to be there." A beat. "I wasn't. And . . . now the world knows something that she wasn't ready to share."

"I'm sure she doesn't—"

His eyes cut to hers, honey hardening to amber. "I fucked up. There's no way to erase that."

Shan was silent for a long moment. "Maybe not," she murmured. "But you can still move forward."

"Yeah. In time."

Her lips twisted. "I know *all* about that."

He squeezed her arm. "I know you do."

"I have to"—she gestured at Rylie—"Pepper has been watching her too much lately."

"Pepper doesn't seem to mind."

"No." Shan smiled. "They're buds. I'm lucky to have her as a friend."

Finn nodded.

She lifted her hand. "Well. I'll just—"

"I'll walk with you."

Not an offer. Also, not exactly a command.

She wasn't sure how she felt about either. All she knew was that it wasn't horrible having Finn at her side as she strode down the beach.

Especially when he said, "If I look pathetic enough, will you make me peanut butter milk to go with this banana bread?"

In fact, her heart leaped, her stomach fluttered, and she laughed loud and outright and freer than she had in ages. "No need to look pathetic," she said. "I already promised Ry earlier."

He fist-pumped.

She grinned.

He brushed a lock of hair out of her face.

Her heart thumped.

And maybe, just maybe, she thought that hope of a brown girl falling for a movie star might not be so far-fetched after all.

"No, Brian," she said into the phone. "Ann can't borrow my car. I'm picking up a few of Rylie's friends after school for a playdate and—"

"Can't you walk?" he interrupted. "Ann's car isn't ready at the shop and she needs to take Billy to his piano lesson."

Her teeth ground together. "I'm taking the girls to the fair. It's too far to walk."

"Do the fair another time." He sighed, a sharp burst of sound through the speaker. "I don't have time for this shit. It's my car. I'll send someone to pick up the keys. Leave them in the office."

A year ago, she would have given in.

To keep the peace, so he wouldn't be mad at her, so . . . no, because she'd been weak and fragile and easily pushed around.

Today?

No.

Hell. No.

"Absolutely not," she snapped. "The title is in *my* name"— she made sure of that after the fucking house fiasco—"and Rylie and I have plans—"

"Don't be such a—"

Her reply was sharp and tipped with ice. "I wouldn't finish that sentence if I were you, Brian Torres."

Silence.

Then, "What is she supposed to do?"

Shannon sighed. "I don't know. Call a Lyft, or a friend, or hell, skip piano for today," she said, tossing up her free hand, even though he couldn't see her. "Ask the dealership for a loner. Do *something.* I don't care, as long as that something doesn't involve me."

"I—"

"This isn't my problem," she interrupted, her tone incredulous, "and I cannot believe you would actually think it was, or expect me to drop everything for the woman you cheated on me with."

"That's not fair—"

She snorted. "I stopped believing in *fair* a long time ago." Just like she'd stopped believing in him. "Figure out your own life, Brian, and leave me to mine."

"I'm traveling—"

She hung up with shaking fingers, both because the anger was fading and also because adrenaline had filled her system, leaving her jittery. She could not believe she'd just done that. She was really freaking proud of herself for *doing it*, took definite pleasure in both cutting him off multiple times, as well as the hanging up . . . but she still couldn't believe she'd done it.

Go her.

She was moving forward, growing some of that spine she wanted to pass on to Ry.

She was making progress. Finally.

"I miss Daddy."

Three words that were the gut punch to end all gut punches.

Because . . . well, Shannon didn't miss Brian anymore. She'd *long* since moved beyond missing her asshole ex-husband.

But she hated that Ry missed him, that Ry missed him being here for these events.

The first day of school.

He'd missed kindergarten.

He was now missing first grade.

God, how had she wasted so many years with such a fucking jerk? The only good thing was that because Ry was in first this year, Shan thought she should be less of a mess than last year.

Less being no tears.

"I know, honey," she said gently. "Your dad wishes he could be here. You know that. He's just really busy at work."

Ry made a face. "He's *always* busy at work."

Yeah. He was.

And with his other family.

Shannon knew that it was only a matter of time before Ry discovered that, and she wanted to shield her daughter from that for as long as possible. But she also knew that someday Ry *would* find out, and her daughter would be hurt, possibly devastated . . . and it would be because Shannon had picked the wrong guy to place her trust in.

Fuck, that was painful.

Her only hope was that she could protect Rylie for as long as possible.

No. Her task wasn't to protect Ry so much as it was for her to make her daughter strong enough to not need Brian in her life. To recognize it would be great to have people in it who cared for her, but that she *didn't* need them to be happy.

Which meant Shan needed to learn how to do the same.

Be thankful for the good people but not desperate. Not build the foundation of her life on someone else's shoulders.

It had to come from her first.

"Let's make a tradition," she said, grabbing Ry's lunchbox from the fridge and helping her zip it into her backpack.

"What's a tradition?"

"It's something special we can do every year on the first day of school. We can get ice cream, or I can make you peanut butter milk, or we can go to the park." Shannon lightly squeezed Rylie's shoulders. "It'll be something fun and special, and just the two of us."

Her daughter's expression screwed up. "Just us?"

She nodded. "Just us."

"Can we go buy socks?"

Shannon's eyes widened. "What?"

"You always say that a pair of cozy socks makes you feel better," Rylie said. "So, I want a pair of cozy socks."

Cozy socks *were* something Shan was addicted to, although they weren't exactly conducive to this beach life.

But her daughter wanted a pair of socks.

She couldn't get Brian here, but she could damn well find Ry the coziest pair of socks on the planet.

"Yeah, baby," she said, standing up. "After school, you and I will go to Sock-a-Palooza"—the tourist sock shop in downtown Stoneybrook—"and we'll find you some cozy socks."

"And you, too, Mommy," she said, slipping her backpack onto her shoulders. "It's your first day of school, too. You need cozy socks."

"Okay." She nodded, grabbed her coffee mug, her own lunchbox. "School. Socks. Pizza for dinner."

"Pizza!" A beat. "With extra pineapple?"

Shan bit back a shudder, considering she was firmly in the camp that pineapple on pizza was disgusting. "Absolutely."

"Yes!" Rylie pushed out the front door. "This is going to be the best day ever!"

Shan followed her, locking up, waving to Finn when she saw him drinking a cup of coffee on his front deck. But they didn't stop, instead turning toward the boardwalk that would take them from the beach and toward school.

They got there early enough for her to see Rylie off to the playground and for her to finish her coffee before the first bell rang.

And then she went out to gather her third graders.

Who were miraculously lined up in the proper spot with mostly smiling faces and non-snotty noses.

No one threw up.

No one had to go to the principal's or forgot their student ID number. No one even talked back.

It *was* the best day ever.

And one that was punctuated by her and Ry scoring matching socks at Sock-a-Palooza that were silky soft and patterned with penguins wearing sunglasses.

It was the best day ever . . . until she walked up to her house and saw the For Sale sign planted in front of it.

TEN

TEARS AND A WHITE COUCH

Finn

HE SAW Rylie and Shannon emerge from the front of her house, walking up the little path that led from the narrow street that all of the cottages' garages backed up to.

He'd taken a dip in the ocean, his towel draped around his shoulders, salt water dripping down his spine in cold rivulets that felt much icier since the sun was setting and the afternoon breeze was picking up.

But one look at Shannon's face and the ice on his spine wasn't from the ocean.

He jogged over. "What is it?"

A shake of her head. A forced smile. "I'm fine."

"Shan—"

"I'm fine."

Sharp now.

A tone that normally would have him backing off. Except . . . the sadness was back. He'd watched it fade to the background over the last week, over peanut butter milk and blue waves. He'd seen it settle as they'd walked by each other on the beach, when he'd brought her a cup of coffee to thank her for the banana bread.

He'd just started to get to know this woman—

And he felt like he was seeing her again for the first time.

Fuck, what had made her so sad?

"I'll see you later, Finn," she said.

"Mom and I are having a tradition."

A twitch of Shan's lips, the sadness still there but tempered by her love for her daughter. "We're making a first day of school tradition."

"Socks and pineapple!" Ry cheered.

More smiling. More sad.

God, he shouldn't care so much. He shouldn't be infatuated with this woman who wasn't even divorced yet, who had her own life to sort out while he was sorting out his. He had his life; she had hers.

He shouldn't care she was sad.

But he did.

"Shan—"

His watch beeped, signaling a call redirected from his cell.

"You should get that," she said, pointing at his watch. "Ry and I will catch up with you another time."

Finn silenced the call. "How was it?"

Brows drawn together. "How was what?"

"How was the first day?" he asked.

"It was awesome," Ry said, dancing around. "I'm in class with my best friend, Lizzy, and Mrs. Montgomery is nice, and I have my own desk organizer with all of my own things in their own spots."

That made him glance up from the dancing child and into Shan's eyes.

Real amusement trumped sad.

"Are you insinuating that because my house is very organized and neat that I have something to do with my child's appreciation of desk caddies?" she asked.

"Yes." A beat. "You have a white couch." His lips twitched. "And matching baskets.

She laughed. "Clearly, that means an obsession with organization."

He lifted a brow. "Am I wrong?"

"No," she admitted, lips curving. "As you well know, since you've set foot in my house." She brushed a hand across his chest.

He froze.

Because her palm sliding across his bare chest . . . fuck, it was the lightest, most innocent touch, and she might as well have slipped her hand in the front of his swim trunks and wrapped her fingers around his cock.

Then she seemed to realize what she'd done and took a hurried step back. "Sorry. I— Uh . . . you had a fly. Um—"

His watch beeped again.

"You should get that," she repeated, skittering back. "Come on, Ry. Our pizza's getting cold."

"Mr. Finn can eat with us," Ry announced.

For the record, Mr. Finn was fine with that. He silenced his watch.

"We're doing our tradition," Shan said. "Remember? Just the two of us."

That was probably the one thing Shannon could have said to get him to not take Rylie up on her offer. Because this was her time with her daughter, and she'd worked all day. Not to mention, she was upset and . . . there was just no way he was going to insert himself into a situation where he didn't belong.

He ruffled Rylie's hair. "We'll do pizza another time," he told her. "This is Mom and Daughter time."

Blue-brown eyes widened. "Oh! Mom and Daughter time is the best! Can I paint my nails to match my new socks?"

Shan chuckled. "Not sure I can manage penguins, sweetheart."

"I meant blue, Mom."

"Well, obviously I can do blue." Shannon winked. "Maybe even sunglasses."

He wanted to see how she could possibly do sunglasses on tiny fingernails. He wanted to eat pizza and see the penguin-printed socks.

But this was Mom and Daughter time.

And his watch buzzed again.

"You really should take care of that," Shannon said, then wrapped an arm around Ry's shoulders and continued walking.

Finn waved, turned for his own house.

Later, he would wish he'd turned the other way, wished he'd gone onto the street and seen the For Sale sign.

He could have put things to rest in a heartbeat.

But he didn't turn the other way.

Instead, he went into his cottage, called his agent back, who was hounding him to make decisions about the piles of scripts.

All were shit.

He picked one anyway.

Then he ordered a pizza of his own.

He was still sitting on his deck, hours later, the sky dark, the sound of the waves constant and soothing, dredges of his pizza on the table in front of him, when he heard it.

Footsteps.

The screech of a chair leg.

Finn turned his head, already knowing what he'd see.

Shannon.

She shook out a blanket, draped it across her lap.

Then went still. So still that if he hadn't known she'd come out onto the deck, hadn't seen her with his own eyes, he wouldn't have known anyone was out there at all.

And he found himself frozen in place, not wanting to break whatever solace she'd found, not wanting to intrude . . . while also wanting, *needing* to study her. To trace her silhouette with his gaze, to note its peaks and valleys highlighted against the moonlight.

What was it about Shannon that was so fascinating?

Was it pure hero complex? Yes, he'd enjoyed and taken pride in the fact that he'd lightened her load, at least for a few days. Was it that he was attracted to her? That was an irrefutable truth. She was beautiful, but he had seen more classically pretty, more curvy, more thin, more tall, more short, more . . . women that could logically be stated fit all of those ideological standards.

Hell, he'd spent the last decade sharing the screen with many of them.

Was it her daughter?

Ry was light to her heavy, bright to her dark, and yet, he'd seen those glimpses of light and bright in Shannon, too. Before life had mostly squashed it out.

Her husband was a dumbass.

He knew that without a doubt.

His pull to Shannon herself? That was a mystery.

One he should probably leave unsolved, and yet, one he also knew he wasn't *going* to leave unsolved.

Especially when he watched her shoulders curl in on themselves, saw her body bend in half, almost crumpling, a sob trailing across the sand to his deck to hit his ears.

He was on his feet and striding toward her before he processed the movement.

Then he was on the bottom step of her deck.

Then he was at her chair.

Her eyes flew up to meet his. "Finn."

He didn't stop to think, didn't say a word. He didn't know what had made her sad that day, couldn't make her ex not be an asshole. The only thing he *could* do was hold her close, let her cry, and then dry her tears when she was finished.

"Finn," she protested when he lifted her in his arms.

The protest died out as he sat down, bringing her flush against his chest, legs stacked across his lap. "Shh," he murmured, wrapping the blanket around her shoulders. "You don't have to tell me why you're crying. Just—just let me hold you while you do."

Silence.

Then a heart-wrenching sob, louder, and so painful that his own heart felt flayed open in response.

Her forehead dropped to his shoulder, tears streaming down her face, soaking into the cotton of his T-shirt. Her arms fell to his waist, and she cried.

Finn held her. For a long, long time, he just held her.

And when the sobs stopped, after he'd wiped her tears from her cheeks, Shannon didn't move from his arms. Just dropped her forehead back to his shoulder and lay limply in his embrace.

So, he continued to hold her.

Until her breathing evened out, until she fell asleep.

He continued to hold her until the moon began to set. He held her until goose bumps lifted on her skin, until she shivered.

Only then did he stop holding her.

But he waited until he'd tucked her under the covers of her bed before he did so.

ELEVEN
PANCAKES

Shannon

"MOM!" Rylie yelled, careening in through the bedroom door and slamming the heavy wooden panel into the wall in the process.

She winced but not as much as she would have if she hadn't installed the plastic disc onto the wall that protected it from rogue knobs—a common occurrence when living with an almost seven-year-old, unfortunately.

This wince came from knowing the wall was safe, but remembering her actions of the night before.

God.

She'd lost it in Finn's arms.

Why had she gotten married so young?

If only she'd gone crazy in college, then she could say her worst memory was a drunken one-night stand with a really jerky guy.

Instead, she'd gotten married to the really jerky guy.

"*Mom!*" Rylie said, coming over and tugging back the blankets. "I want pancakes before school. And Mr. Finn wants them, too."

Shan froze. "Mr. Finn?"

"Uh-huh. He was asleep on the couch, but I woke him up." She spun in a circle. "Do you like my outfit? Lizzy and I are going to match today."

"Wait, Ry." Shan sat up, pushing off the bed. "Mr. Finn—*er* Finn is here? Why?"

"Silly! You let Mr. Finn stay on the couch because he got locked out of his house." Ry's face screwed up. "He's going to call a . . . doors man to let him in."

"A locksmith?"

"Yeah. A locksmith." Rylie nodded firmly. "So, can we have pancakes, Mommy?"

Shannon's eyes flicked to the clock, saw that unfortunately they had plenty of time for her to shower, dress, *and* still make pancakes.

"Mr. Finn is on the couch?"

"Nope," Ry said. "He's on the deck."

"Okay, honey. I'll make pancakes. But I need to shower first."

"Yes! Pancakes!" Rylie ran off then skidded to a stop at the bedroom door. "I'm going to wear my new socks today. Are you?"

"Sure, baby."

Then she was off, yelling, "Mom said yes for pancakes, but she needs to shower!"

Shan quickly pulled together an outfit and brought it into the bathroom with her, taking the world's quickest shower because there was something unnerving . . . okay, she would be lying if she said it was *only* unnerving to picture Finn standing on the deck, knowing she was naked under a stream of water.

Would he like what he saw?

Making a disgusted noise, she yanked the knob to the right, shutting off the water and then stepping out of the stall.

Her body was fine. She was thin with some curves, but she also had stretch marks from Ry's pregnancy, and her boobs were . . . well, they'd had their perkier days. And Finn filmed movies with gorgeous actresses and models, women who probably didn't have stretch marks—or even if they *did* have them, then they at least had a team of makeup artists, wardrobe people, and lighting technicians to make them look their best.

She was—

"Yeah, no," she muttered, meeting her eyes in the mirror. "I'm so not doing this."

She tugged on her favorite pair of jeans, the ones that hugged her not-so-Hollywood curves but made her ass look fabulous. She added a pale blue blouse that brought out the color of her eyes, put on her new penguin socks, slipped into her favorite and ridiculously expensive but comfortable flats, then slapped some minimal makeup onto her face, threw on a necklace, swiped a brush through her hair, and called it good.

Long ago, she'd given up wearing anything really nice and expensive (her shoes aside, since she needed her feet to be comfortable in order to get through the day), even though her third graders were neater than the kindergartners she'd begun her teaching career with, it had only taken one experience with glitter, white glue, and feathers to teach her that lesson.

Also, let it be noted that she no longer used glitter in her classes either.

She tossed her towel in the hamper, along with her jammies, and left the bathroom.

Pancake time.

Correction: girding her loins against Finn Stoneman time.

He was standing in the hall, leaning back against the wall, his head perfectly placed between her wedding picture and one of her and Ry—two guesses for which picture she was wishing she'd shit-canned in that moment, and it wasn't the one that had her and her daughter in matching flowy dresses, waves crashing over their ankles.

He smiled. "Morning."

"Why'd you sleep on my couch?"

The smile faltered, and seriously, she got it. Her tone was sharp, but that was mostly because the man was fucking ridiculous.

How in the hell did someone look so sexy this early in the morning, after sleeping on her couch, without changing his clothes or brushing his teeth? How did he look so freaking sexy standing in her hallway, slightly rumpled, stubble on his cheeks . . . and she repeated. Too. Fucking. Sexy.

Ugh.

He pushed off the wall and came close.

Close enough that his spicy scent washed over her. Close enough that she felt the heat of his chest through the thin material of her blouse. Close enough that she could see he had a ring of gray in those honey-colored eyes.

He brushed his thumb lightly over her cheek.

Shan's lips parted, breath catching.

"Not swollen," he murmured.

"Wh-what?"

"Your eyes are the same gorgeous blue as always," he said. "Not swollen. Not red."

That thumb drifted lower, brushing over her jaw, drifting along her bottom lip.

"I—uh—"

"I slept on your couch because you and Rylie were asleep, and I didn't know where your spare key was."

She frowned.

"So I could lock up."

More frowning.

His thumb dipped lower, sliding forward, bringing his palm in contact with her skin as he cupped the side of her neck. "Because after I put you in your bed, I wasn't going to leave you and Rylie asleep in an unlocked house."

"But this is Stoneybrook."

One brow came up. "And is Stoneybrook a fictional utopia where nothing bad ever happens?"

"No," she admitted.

"So, I wasn't leaving you unprotected."

"Finn, the worst thing that has happened in the last couple of years is Pepper nearly getting mowed down by an old lady because that old lady was trying to read the sign Pepper was holding and got distracted." Her lips twitched. "But that's Pepper's Chaos Magnet—her words, not mine."

"Pepper's Chaos Magnet." He grinned. "Yeah, that's fitting."

She shrugged. "See? You could have easily left."

"No, I couldn't have."

A huff.

"There was no way I was leaving you and Ry vulnerable," he said mulishly. "So, just drop it, okay?"

"No, I will not drop it," she snapped. "You have your own life. I don't need you to rescue me or—"

He bent and slanted his lips across hers.

Morning breath.

He should have had morning breath.

That was the only logical thought that went through her mind before his mouth settled on hers, before his tongue drifted across the seam of her lips, and slipped inside, before she tasted him—coffee and mint. Before that tongue slid against hers and she got lost in the feel of him.

Two men.

She'd kissed two men in her life.

Brian.

Finn.

And this was like her first time all over again.

Heat slid down her spine, not in an explosion, but rather in a licking, consuming forest fire, burning slowly, combusting everything in its path. Flames coalescing and spreading outward along her skin, up her nape, drifting down to her thighs, in between.

Slow. Ever-increasing. Incineration.

And what a way to go.

But then Finn lifted his head, removed his hand from her throat.

"What—"

Rylie appeared in the hall. "Mom! Pancakes!"

Shannon shook herself. "Get the bowl, baby. I'll be right there. Finn—"

He kissed her again.

This time wasn't slow. It was a sparked fire from lightning, flames exploding from the simplest contact. Lips immediately parting, her hands gripping his shoulders, sliding up into his hair, her body flush against him.

Finn growled, arms banding tightly around her, one hand sliding to her ass and tugging her hips to his, the other sliding up to her hair, tilting her head until their mouths met in a perfect frenzy of teeth and tongues and lips. She moaned and arched against him, her pelvis coming into contact with the hard jut of his erection, and fuck, if she didn't see actual stars from this man's mouth, his body, his cock.

Eventually, though, they needed to breathe.

They both pulled back, chests heaving.

Finn cupped her cheek. "I should apologize for taking advantage of you," he said, and added, right over her when she began protesting, "I only came back to tell you that you didn't have to cook for me." He brushed his lips over hers. "So, I should say I'm sorry for kissing you." Another brush. "But I'm not going to. Not when I've been dreaming about doing it from the moment I first saw you." One final brush before he dropped his hands and stepped away. "There is no fucking way I'm going to apologize for the best kiss of my life."

Then he turned and walked down the hall, disappearing into the kitchen, leaving her standing there, reeling.

For two huge, ginormous, *astronomical* reasons.

One, dreaming about *her*?

And two, the best kiss of his life?

The. Best. Kiss. Of *his* life?

Finn popped his head out of the kitchen, lips slightly swollen as they curved up into that gorgeous, award-winning smile.

"Come on down, Blue Eyes," he called. "I made coffee."

He disappeared.

And she stood there for a few more seconds, still reeling. Only this time, it was for a third reason.

The third being: he'd made coffee?

Really?

"Pancakes!"

Shannon shook herself and hightailed it into the kitchen, getting her butt into gear so she could make them all pancakes and she and Ry would not be late for the second day of school.

The pancakes weren't her best.

But Ry and Finn devoured them anyway.

Then Finn gave her a fourth reason for continuing to reel— he demanded her spare key . . . and to do the dishes.

Maybe that was five reasons?

Either way, she and Rylie were out the door right on time,

Ry's lunchbox in her backpack, *her* lunchbox in hand, along with a to-go cup of coffee in the other.

All Finn's doing while she'd been making the mediocre pancakes.

The man was . . .

Unbelievable.

And for the record, while she might have made middling pancakes, Finn's coffee was anything but.

She took a sip of the hot, steaming beverage as she and Ry walked to school, listening to her daughter prattle on about some imaginary game she and Lizzy were going to play, all while wondering if it was the coffee that was outstanding . . . or if it was because Finn had made it.

Because Finn had been more of a partner in forty-minutes that morning, in a few moments over the course of a week, than Brian ever had been.

She knew she'd been missing a lot.

She'd just never known precisely how much until she'd met Finn.

"I'M NOT sure I can make this happen, Shannon," Alberto said, resignation in his tone as she sat across his desk.

He'd asked her to come by his office after school and she'd just assumed that it was good news, that he'd been able to finagle some deal with Brian and the house, but the defeated expression on his face told her otherwise.

Shit.

She was going to have to move and—

No.

God, enough.

Why should she have to uproot hers and Rylie's lives, just because he couldn't keep his dick in his pants?

"I asked for one thing," she said, steel in her tone. "One. Thing."

Alberto sighed. "It's a big thing, all other issues aside."

"No child support. No alimony. No retirement. No bank account. *I* pay the mortgage. *I'm* paying for his auto loan—"

"I didn't advise any of that," Alberto said. "In fact, it's against my advice—"

"One thing," she repeated.

Alberto sighed.

"He agreed," she said. "He promised."

"Promises aren't always—"

Her fist came down on her thigh, the loud *smack* filling the room. "I know *all* about promises and how they aren't always kept, but I don't care about any of the other promises Brian gave me." She exhaled. "None of them . . . except for one that enables me to keep this house."

"I could possibly file—" He broke off, started making notes on his legal pad.

"Do it," she said, reaching across the desk and covering his hand with hers. "Fight for me. I know I'm paying you to be on my side, to have my back, to protect me and Rylie, but please, you have to know this isn't right. I need you to help me find my way through."

Resignation was replaced with resolve. "I'm going to find a way through for you, Shan."

"With the house?"

His mouth flattened out. "I'll throw everything I have at him."

"That's all I'm asking."

They discussed a few more things then Shannon shook his hand and said her goodbyes, knowing that while Alberto hadn't promised the house at the end of this process, that he *had* promised to fight.

And she was starting to realize maybe it was less about winning and more about that fight.

Stand up for herself.

Demand what she deserved.

Because if she didn't, then who would?

TWELVE

SCRUNCHY FACES BRING THE BIG BUCKS

Finn

"YOU REALLY DIDN'T HAVE to bring us dinner," Shannon said for about the tenth time since he'd shown up about thirty minutes earlier, BBQ burgers with extra bacon and barbeque sauce in hand for the adults, chicken fingers and applesauce for Rylie.

He might have asked Pepper for intel.

He might have also brought mint chocolate chip milkshakes because those were apparently Shannon and Rylie's favorite.

"You've fed me multiple times already," he said. Again. "Least I can do is bring you takeout one time."

She made a face, but at least she stopped arguing with him.

Part of that might be because Rylie was happily slurping her milkshake and chowing down on her "Chicken nuggies!" as she'd called them. Apparently "nuggies" were Baby Yoda's favorite as well, and since Lizzy had an older brother who was into *Star Wars*, Lizzy was into *Star Wars*, and because Lizzy and Rylie were best friends for life—two days in elementary school was sometimes a lifetime—now Rylie was into all things green and space-related.

And somehow, he'd followed all of that the first time Shannon had explained it.

The other reason she might have stopped arguing with him was because she'd finally taken a bite of her burger.

Finn could attest to their tastiness.

Juicy. Firm. Just the right amount of sauce.

And now his dick was hard.

Cool.

He inwardly rolled his eyes, forcing his thoughts to the ocean, to the bad scripts, to his agent explaining that things were blowing over and he could head back to L.A. soon.

Finn didn't *want* to go to L.A.

He liked it here in Stoneybrook. He liked sitting on his deck and watching the waves—not that he couldn't do that in L.A. It was just that . . . this wasn't Hollywood. Aside from the one selfie request he'd had on the beach, no one bothered him or approached. No pictures had appeared in magazines or online. He could walk down the street and pick up takeout without it being a shit show of pushy paparazzi. And . . . he liked Shannon. He liked Rylie. He liked being close enough to chat with Pepper or to veer off from human contact altogether and go take a dip in the ocean.

But mostly, he liked the person he was with Shannon.

He liked thinking about someone else.

He loved getting out of his head.

He—

"Why's your face all scrunchy, Mr. Finn?" Rylie asked around a bite of *nuggies.*

"Rylie!" Shan exclaimed.

Finn smothered a grin. "You know you can just call me Finn?" he said, instead of answering Ry about the face-scrunching. Mostly because he wasn't going to admit to thinking about nuggies, but also because he thought that if he told Shannon he liked her a lot and was considering leaving L.A. in the dust and making a home base in Stoneybrook—preferably right next door if he could convince the owner of the house he was staying at to sell or rent long-term—he was pretty sure she'd run screaming for the hills.

If *he* thought about it for too long, he almost considered running for the hills.

But here was the thing . . . he'd spent years—years!—having every step of his life and career planned out for him.

Filming schedules, promotion, supposed spontaneous carpool sing-a-long participation, cover shoots, even the few times he'd gotten to take a vacation had been planned out by his publicist so as to minimize the media presence.

He hadn't been able to just walk down the street without a security guard in years.

But in Stoneybrook, he could sit on his deck and just be.

Finn was here because he'd needed to get away from L.A., because he'd needed to get his paparazzi-drawing presence away from his family.

But he was also here because he wasn't happy.

"Pepper!" Ry spun in her chair, not answering him about the whole just Finn thing. "Mom! It's Pepper! Can I go say hi?"

Shan glanced across the beach and he followed suit, seeing Pepper on her deck, who caught sight of them and waved.

Shannon's lips twitched. "Just a quick hello. Derek just got back into town, and I'm sure they want some time alone." A beat. "Plus, you have nuggies to finish!"

"Nuggies!" Ry yelled, charging across the sand.

"She doesn't move in anything but a sprint, does she?" he asked.

A shake of Shan's head, lips curving further. "Nope," she

said. "Heaven help her teacher. I've already invested in a case of wine for her for Teacher Appreciation Week."

"Isn't that in May?"

"I'm impressed you know that, Mr. Finn."

He snorted. "My mom is a teacher. It was ingrained in me to know."

"Good son."

"Good *mom*," he challenged.

"I think that, too," she said softly.

They sat in quiet for a couple minutes, gazes on Pepper and Rylie and then, he was guessing, Derek, when a man walked out from the inside of Pepper's house, a platter of food in his hand. His guess was confirmed when he heard Rylie shout, "Derek!" and throw her arms around his waist.

Shannon shifted next to him, capturing her dark brown hair in one hand and sweeping it up into a ponytail, making her soft floral scent drift through the air and up to his nose as they watched Derek hand the food off to Pepper and sweep Ry up into the air. "I'm lucky to have them," she murmured. "That Ry has them in her life."

"Pepper is good people," he agreed, taking a bite of his burger. "And seeing how happy she's been, I'm guessing Derek is, too."

"He is," Shan said and then surprised him by asking, "So, are you going to share with the class what was making you have that scrunchy expression earlier, *Mr.* Finn?"

"I resent the term scrunchy," he deflected.

"Finn."

Teacher voice.

She was giving him teacher voice . . . and it worked. He shifted to meet her gaze. "Yeah?"

But apparently, Shannon only used her powers for good

because, when his eyes hit hers, she said, face soft, "You really don't have to tell me."

He set down his burger. "Do you ever feel like you're surrounded by people all day but are somehow still all alone?"

She froze, a fry clutched between her fingers, mouth falling open.

He shook himself. Of course, she didn't. He was just off and in his head. "Sorry," he muttered. "I shouldn't have said that. Ignore me. I'm just in a weird mood."

"It's not"—she set down her own burger, wiped her hand on her napkin, then rested it on the back of his—"that. It's just— I've felt that way *so* much over the last few years."

He froze.

"Tell me why you feel alone," she said gently.

"It's ridiculous," he muttered. "No one wants to hear a movie star complain." A shrug. "I have enough money that if I'm lonely, I can pay people to be my friends if needed."

"But why would you have to?"

"Or want to," he qualified. A sigh. "Which is probably why I'm alone."

"No girlfriend?"

He lifted a brow. "I wouldn't have kissed you if I had one."

"Oh—" Her cheeks pinkened. "I—I wasn't sure how those things worked in Hollywood. Everything seems so . . ."

"Fake?"

She nodded.

"Some of it is," he agreed. "But a lot of it is real. It's just . . . sometimes a relationship is a recipe for disaster when us actors spend most of our day-to-day lives being catered to our every whim. You either get two giant egos together, who both have been infantilized into not even being able to get themselves a cup of coffee, or you have one giant ego, and that's a feat to put up with."

"You seem to do fine getting your own coffee."

He chuckled. "Luckily, my family helps me keep my head straight."

"But you still feel alone?"

A shrug. "It's fine. I'm one of the few people to make it."

"Just because you're successful doesn't mean you're supposed to be happy all the time."

"That's not what most people think," he said. "And look, I get it. Most of my workdays are spent in hair and makeup, with my assistant handling my schedule, keeping me on track, and a PA bringing me food as I work beside beautiful people." He sat back in his chair. "I have five homes around the world. I have eight cars and can charter a private jet when I want to go somewhere. I've taken care of my family. I *am* lucky. I've been given a gift, so I *should* be happy."

"But you're not."

"It's not that so much as . . ." He faltered for a moment. "People want a piece of me all day, every day—a smile, a picture, a performance, those are easy. It's the others that are harder— money, favors, introductions, networking opportunities. How do you choose one and not the other? And then with my sister, that fucker raped her, and you know what he did afterward when he found out she was related to me?"

Anger made his teeth grind together, fury burning down his spine.

Shan squeezed his hand.

"He tried to blackmail her. Demanding she pay him off or he'd tell the world he'd fucked Finn Stoneman's sister and she liked it."

His hands were clenched into fists, the fucking memory of that bastard and his threats after he'd violated and taken something so precious from Finn's sister, making him want to punch something. Preferably, the fucker's face over and over and *over* again until it was transformed into pulp, until Finn's knuckles were split open and he was drenched in the blood of the man who'd hurt his sister.

Too far?

Probably.

But he'd never stop wishing that anyway.

And the fucker had taken a plea bargain, was going to be in jail for the next three years.

"Three years," he said. "The bastard got *three years*. My sister will never, *ever* be the same, and he'll be out in eighteen months with good behavior."

"I—" Shan reached out and covered his other hand so that both of hers were on top of his. "I'm sorry. I'm sorry that disgusting excuse for a human did that to your sister. I'm sorry the world doesn't seem to care about women and their bodies when they're violated and hurt but cares too much when women want to make choices about their health and their bodies." She sighed. "But most of all, I'm just terribly sorry your sister will be marked by this forever."

"Thank you." He forced his fists to flatten out, to press into the arms of his chair, for his lungs to suck in a slow, even breath. "It just . . . it put things into perspective for me. I've been unhappy and lonely because of my big, movie star life, and she's . . . been devastated."

"Finn." Her chair screeched on the deck as she shifted to face him more fully. "Look at me."

He found it impossible to not look at her.

Even though he still felt deep shame at not being able to protect his sister, at having exposed what was done to her to the media, even though the urge to crawl back into his own skin and hide was intense, Finn couldn't keep his eyes from hers.

"This is not your fault."

"I—"

"Bad stuff happens. People make mistakes. You're not immune to that, even if you make millions of dollars on a movie set."

"But—"

"And just because you make a lot of money doesn't mean you're not allowed to be sad or lonely or depressed." She cupped his cheek. "Just because you're a movie star doesn't mean you're not allowed to feel. Beneath it all, you're just a normal human being."

He covered her hand with his. "How'd you get to be so smart?"

Lips tipped up, and he wanted to kiss her again. Except they were in full view of Pepper and Rylie. Except, he didn't know if she *wanted* him to kiss her again, most especially in front of her daughter and friends.

She wasn't divorced yet.

Her husband was an ass.

"Six years of college and copious amounts of continuing ed," she said, answering his rhetorical question with a chuckle, and leaning back slightly.

He released her palm that was pressed to his cheek, hating the feel of her hand sliding away, hating that her other hand followed suit, hating that the connection was broken, that this little circle of peace they'd built around themselves was disturbed.

"Go on a date with me," he blurted.

Shan had picked up her burger, was bringing it to her mouth. At his blurt, she froze, mouth open in what would have gotten a huge audience laugh if it had been a scene in one of his movies.

He had to admit that being on the receiving end of it in real life didn't feel great.

Her "*What?*" even less so.

"Never mind," he said quickly. Dumbass. She was still married, still pulling the pieces of her life back together. "Forget—"

"You'd want to go on a date with *me?*"

He frowned at the incredulity in her tone. "Why are you saying it like that?"

"What do you mean, why am I saying it like that?" she said. "You're a huge movie star. I'm me. *Of course,* I'm saying it like that."

"You're a beautiful, smart, funny woman. *Of course,* I want the privilege of taking you on a date."

She laughed.

Literally bent in half, chest falling toward her knees, burger still clutched in her hand as near-hysterical laughter filled the space around her.

"You— Me—" Giggles erupted, but he didn't find it the least bit funny.

"Shannon."

Her head came up. "Me." A shake of that head. "*Me.* An average brown girl with a movie star."

"Shan—"

"Me. A soon-to-be-divorced single mom with the *biggest* movie star in the world."

"I—"

"*Me.*" She shook her head again. "With *the* Finn."

He sighed, knew he wasn't going to talk her into believing that he wanted to take her out on a date, to see if this rapport they had, if the connection that had formed was real and would continue to grow.

Finn needed a call to action.

He tugged the burger out of Shannon's hands and tossed it on the paper wrapper she'd spread on the table.

She stopped laughing.

He stood.

She bit her lip.

He tugged her into his arms.

She released a shuddering breath.

"Yes," he murmured. "*You*. With *the* Finn."

Then he lowered his head and slanted his mouth across hers. Wide eyes met his for a moment before her lids slid closed, before she melted in his arms, before her lips parted, and . . . she kissed him back.

Hand sliding up his arms, resting on his shoulders, moving in and weaving into the hair on his nape, her nails lightly raking his skin.

Heat.

Goose bumps.

This woman.

He pulled her more tightly against him, loving the way her scent fluttered up and flowed over him, her soft moan in the back of her throat as she leaned more heavily against him.

"Mom! Mr. Finn is kissing you!" Rylie yelled, words punctuating her footsteps on the deck.

Shannon lurched from his arms, feeling like she yanked out half of the hairs from his scalp in the process. Finn sucked in a breath, resisting the urge to tug her back against him, to kiss her again, to watch her melt, feel her lips and tongue against his.

But Rylie was there.

He turned and squatted down in front of her. "I *was* kissing your mom."

Shannon made a choking sound.

"Is that okay with you?"

Rylie tilted her head to the side, brown-blue eyes studying him closely. "Do you like her?"

"Ry—" Shannon gasped. "That—"

"I do," he said, meeting that gaze straight on. "I think your mom is pretty great."

Rylie nodded. "She *is* great."

"So is it okay with you if I kiss her?"

"My dad never did," she said.

Finn struggled to absorb that gut punch, to not look over at Shannon when she made a pained noise. "If she wants me to kiss her, then your mom deserves to be kissed." More clunky words. But the next he spouted at least made more sense. "She deserves to be happy."

"I know." Her response was laced with the nonchalance of a seven-year-old, especially as her eyes drifted from his to the remains of her meal on the table. A nod. "If it makes her happy, then you can kiss her."

She scooped up a nugget and took off for the sand, just enough sun left in the sky for her to add another turret to her sandcastle masterpiece, but skittered to a stop on the bottom step. "Mr. Finn?"

"Yeah?"

"If it makes her happy, you can marry my mom, too."

The nugget went into her mouth, and she took off for her sandcastle.

Finn straightened, slowly turned back to face Shannon, seeing her expression was as shell-shocked as he felt.

From the kiss.

From Ry's matter-of-fact declaration.

From, at least on his part, the notion that the almost-seven-year-old's idea might not be the worst one.

He saw a flash of red hair in his periphery, knew that Pepper was watching, that she and Derek were probably documenting the event for posterity . . . and for Pepper's part, to tease Finn later.

But he didn't care.

There was only one question he wanted the answer to.

"Does it?" he asked softly.

Wide blue eyes met his, a trace of panic in their depths.

"Do my kisses make you happy?"

No, he wasn't proposing marriage. Yes, he liked her. Yes, he was considering setting up a home base in Stoneybrook to be closer to her and Rylie.

But, marriage?

No. Not yet, anyway.

But not yet isn't a no, Finn. That mental voice was his mother's. The same one that always infiltrated his inner thoughts. Part ensuring he stayed on task. Part *calling* him to task. But also never failing to help him get his thoughts in order.

"Shannon?" he asked when she stared at him without speaking.

She shook herself.

"Do you?"

"Do I what?"

"Do you like it when I kiss you?" A beat. "Or, in Ry's words, does it make you happy?"

White teeth nibbling on a pink bottom lip. "I—" She sighed, gaze coming to his. "Yes, Finn. I like it when you kiss me."

Relief.

Sweet, sweet relief.

But also awareness that she hadn't answered his other question, about it making her happy. Instinctively, Finn knew the time for that conversation could come later, when she wasn't so unnerved, when Pepper and Derek weren't watching, when their dinner wasn't getting cold.

So, he tugged her back into her chair, handed over her burger, and then he asked her about her second day of school.

Shy.

Shy at first, but then she found her rhythm, quickly having

him in stitches about a kindergartner who'd been confident enough to climb the outside of the play structure while she was taking her turn supervising midday recess, but hadn't been confident enough to get down.

"And finally, the custodian managed to find the tall ladder and we got him down." She chuckled. "But I could have sworn that I was going to have to call the fire department."

"They did have to call the fire department for me once," he said.

"What?"

His lips twitched and he told her a story he'd never shared with anyone, about filming on location in Scotland a few years back, with a small crew he'd since sworn to secrecy.

"Then the director convinced me to climb down the cliff."

She gasped.

"I had a safety line," he said. "It was perfectly safe." A beat. "Except for the fact that I'd packed on thirty pounds of muscle for the role and every time I tried to pull my heavy ass back up the rocky side, the stones crumbled and fell apart in my hands."

Another gasp.

"There were five of us that day." He shook his head, remembering how helpless he'd felt. "And I think that all together they weighed less than me at that time. They couldn't get me up, so we had to call the fire brigade."

"Brigade?"

"We were in a remote part of Scotland at the time," he explained. "They had me back up in minutes, and I swear I spent a fortune on Scottish whiskey for them *and* the crew in order to keep their silence."

"That's blackmail."

"Blackmail I was willing to pay in order to confiscate their phones and delete the videos and pictures they took that day."

She laughed, eyes dancing. "I bet that was quite a sight to

see."

"I imagine it was."

Her head tilted.

"What?"

"I'm trying to imagine you with thirty more pounds of muscle," she said, tone teasing. "You must have been huge."

"Words a man dreams of hearing," he deadpanned.

She swatted him. "You know what I mean."

He waggled his brows. "I sure do."

"Oh, my God."

"Yes."

A groan and he leaned over his chair, brushed his lips over hers. "What will I have to pay in order for you to keep your silence about my story?"

"Hmm."

Calculation in bright blue eyes, and Finn braced himself almost without realizing it, the slice of uncertainty drifting forward unbidden, because even though they were laughing and joking around, *this* was the point that most people asked for big things. Things he *could* give, but requests that were often more than he *wanted* to give.

"You'll bring me a mug of coffee sometime," she finally said. "However you made it this morning, you'll replicate that and bring me one large mug with extra cream."

"Coffee?" he repeated. "That's it?"

She shrugged. "That's it."

Relief.

Respect.

Like. Fuck, he liked this woman a lot.

They finished eating, exchanging more war stories, though this time none of them included the fire brigade, then they packed up the garbage, and she called Rylie in for homework and bath time, admitting with a chagrined look that she had some tweaks she needed to make to her lesson plans based on a few "surprises" from her class. Finn read that as she had a couple of challenging students under her charge, but when he asked, she just shrugged and said, "Meh. It's just part of the job."

"Superhero," he murmured.

She rolled her eyes. "Not so much." Her eyes darted away then back to his. "Thanks again for dinner."

He nodded.

She nibbled at that bottom lip.

"Can I kiss you goodnight?"

Shy eyes on his, but what made his heart skip a beat was the lack of sadness within those blue depths.

After spending the evening with him.

Yeah, that felt good.

What felt better?

Her mouth against his. Her body pressed flush to his. Her tongue, her lips, her arms wrapping tight around his neck.

Yeah, *all* that was better.

So much better that the second he walked into his cottage, he pulled out his cell and told his assistant when he picked up the call to, "buy me a house on this beach as quickly as possible. I don't care how much it costs," he added when his assistant sputtered. "I just want it done as quickly as possible."

Then he hung up and went to sit on his deck, listening to the waves as darkness fell around him.

For the first time in years, he'd finally found peace.

For the first time in years, he'd finally found something he wanted to pursue and ferret out and explore further.

For the first time in years, he was excited to see what life would hand him.

Unfortunately, what Finn didn't realize was exactly what that call had set in motion.

THIRTEEN
THIRTY POUNDS OF MUSCLE

Shannon

THE NEXT MORNING there was a cup of coffee waiting on her front deck.

It was held by a world-famous movie star, but that was no big deal.

Ha.

Who was she kidding?

It was a thousand times better because it was held by *the* Finn.

"Morning," he said, extending the cup.

"Morning," she murmured, taking it and bringing it up to her lips for one glorious sip. "Oh my God," she moaned. "You're the best ever." She took another sip, moaned again.

"Killing me, sweetheart," he said softly.

"Wh—" She glanced from the cup to his face and felt her cheeks go hot. "*Oh.* I—"

Rylie barreled from the kitchen, her princess backpack on her shoulders, but an old *Star Wars* shirt of Shannon's draped over her body like a dress, black leggings beneath, pink sparkly sneakers on her feet.

Her daughter loved clothes.

No clue where she got that from.

Another *ha*, Shan thought as she glanced down at her own sparkly flats, black jeans, floral blouse, and jumble of necklaces.

"Mr. Finn!"

"Ms. Rylie!" He pulled out another to-go cup and handed it to her. This one was bedazzled with rhinestones spelling out "Princess."

"Coffee?" Ry asked excitedly.

"Nice try." He ruffled her hair. "Hot chocolate." His eyes flicked to Shannon's and he murmured, "Sorry, I should have asked first."

She smiled. "It's fine."

"Chocolate is the best!" Ry said on a fist pump.

"From the mouths of babes," Shannon said, stepping out onto the deck, shutting and locking the doors behind her. "Sorry to rush you out. But we have to leave, or we'll be late."

Finn nodded. "I figured I'd walk with you."

She froze.

"Unless that's not okay . . ." His words trailed off.

"Um . . . no, that's fine. It's great. Uh—"

He bent, brushed his lips across hers. "Don't overthink it," he murmured. "I just wanted to see you."

"You—" Another kiss, and as he straightened, releasing her lips slowly, her breath caught, his skin gilded gold by the morning sun. "You're pretty in the morning," she murmured.

He kissed the tip of her nose. "So are you." A moment passed. "So, is me walking with you okay?"

Was it?

Shan wasn't sure, but . . . she also didn't want to walk without him.

Ugh.

She was torn, and she *shouldn't* be torn. This was Finn. He'd brought her dinner the night before and coffee this morning. Hell, he'd brought Ry hot chocolate in a bedazzled cup. She should be jumping with joy at his interest in her. But she'd liked Brian so much, had cared for him and loved him with everything inside of her, and now she was feeling . . . a lot.

For Finn.

And that was fucking scary.

No, it was terrifying.

Unfortunately—because she didn't want to hurt his feelings —he could see that. "You know what?" he said. "I'll just see you guys around another time. Maybe dinner later in the week—"

She had a decision to make.

To continue being scared, to keep living this half-life of hers.

Or she could grasp onto this scary newness in front of her and just . . . live.

Finn stepped away, but she lurched forward, laced her hand with his. "No," she said. "I mean, yes, to dinner later in the week. No, to you leaving. I'd be happy to have an adult to walk with." She smiled, albeit a bit nervously. "We meet Lizzy on the way and then my life is sparkles and *Star Wars*."

"*Star Wars!*" Ry exclaimed, bustling down the stairs, her backpack bouncing.

"That," Shan confirmed.

"So, I shouldn't mention to her that I've worked with Rey on a film that's coming out next year."

"Uh, no," she said. "Because she doesn't have any concept of a film's release date and will want to see it immediately."

"I happen to have a copy."

She sighed. "Of course you do."

"But it's not exactly kid-friendly."

"No?" she asked, rounding the house with him beside her.

"Nope," he said. "Mostly because it features me and my extra thirty pounds of muscle shirtless for most of the film."

"Hmm. So, how soon until I can watch it?"

He grinned. "Tonight?" he asked. "I actually *do* need to watch it. I promised the director I'd review this cut."

"You're shirtless for most of it?"

Still smiling. "Yup."

"Nope." She shook her head. "I don't think I could put myself through the torture."

He made an affronted noise, started to joke back, but she missed it. Mostly because the realtor sign was gone. Just as quickly as it had appeared and upended her emotions, it was gone again. She pulled out her cell, and sent a text to Alberto, letting him know it was gone.

Strange.

But the sign being gone was good, right?

That meant her call to the lawyer the night before had actually done something, that he'd been able to work his magic.

Relief poured through her.

"Shan?"

Or maybe, Brian had found some humanity and dropped the issue. Although, more likely, Alberto had drummed up some of the lawyer mojo she paid him for and had stopped the sale in its tracks.

Thank God.

"Shannon?" Finn asked. "Are you okay?"

She shook herself, glanced down at her watch, knowing she didn't have any more time to delay if she wanted to make it to school on time. "I'm fine." She smiled. "Sorry, I was wool-gathering."

"About?"

"My—"

"Mom! Can I run up and join Lizzy?" Ry shouted, taking several steps in that direction.

"No!" she called back. "Wait for me."

Then she hustled after her bouncing-in-place daughter, catching up with her before Ry lost patience and darted across a street or driveway where someone might be backing out and not see her.

As she moved, she forgot about Brian and the For Sale sign. In fact, as they caught up with Lizzy, also clad in *Star Wars* gear, as they made it through the madness of school drop-off and playground supervision, and as Finn walked her to her classroom, stepping inside the door and out of sight of the nosy-nellies to brush a kiss across her lips, she completely forgot all about their woolgathering conversation in the first place.

Later, she would wish she hadn't.

But in that moment, she cherished her tingling lips and just waved goodbye.

"What are the chances of you putting on thirty pounds of muscle again?" she said, after pausing the movie like Finn had asked.

"Zero." He glanced up from his cell, where he was taking notes about the film he'd brought over for them to watch after Rylie had gone to bed. "I didn't see a carb for outside of six months. There is absolutely no way I could ever do that again."

Her lips twitched. "Until the next role calls for it."

A sheepish grin. "Okay, so you're probably right. If the conditions were right, I *could* do it. But let it be known I was a grumpy asshole during the entire shoot."

"If I wasn't eating carbs, I'd feel the same way." She took a sip of wine from her glass. "This is really good, by the way."

"The wine or the movie?"

She snorted. "Well, since you somehow figured out my favorite type of wine"—she paused, waiting to see if he'd dish on how he'd figured that out, but when he didn't, she went on, keeping her own suspicions for how (or *whom*—cough, Pepper) to herself—"I'd have to say the wine."

He narrowed his eyes.

"But just note, the movie is all right, too."

"A ringing endorsement," he deadpanned.

There was something about his tone . . . Shan set her wine down and shifted on the couch, facing him fully. "You do know this film is incredible, right?"

"It's good," he said, shrugging as he made another note then set his phone on the table. "But it's not going to change people's lives."

Hmm.

"And is that what you want to do?" she asked carefully. "To change people's lives?"

Silence.

Then, "I know it makes me sound like a selfish, egotistical asshole, but, yes. I do."

"I don't think that's necessarily a bad thing," she said. "I mean, there's a part of me that wants to know I'm doing something important and valuable."

"You're teaching America's youth. I don't think you have to go far to find your value."

"Maybe." She sat back. "But many times I sit back and wonder if I'm doing enough. If I've used my platform effectively to really help them become well-adjusted, good people. Or if it's all pointless in the end because the world is so harsh and unforgiving and many of them will turn out to be assholes anyway."

Finn tilted his head to the side, studying her for a long time.

Long enough that she felt guilty for calling her students future assholes.

But then he took her hand, laced their fingers together. "I'm supposed to be the one with the words." A soft chuckle. "Though, I guess that they're usually written for me, so it shouldn't be a surprise."

"What are you talking about?"

"You always are able to articulate aloud the words I don't know I'm thinking."

She frowned.

"Did you know that I chose my latest project by closing my eyes and picking from the pile of scripts—well, emails with scripts attached—at random?"

"Um—"

"And that it's shit. Not because of the writing or even the story, but because I couldn't see myself in the role. Nothing felt original or fresh or new, and it hasn't for years."

"I'm not sure I know what you mean," she said.

"My favorite part of acting has always been trying on someone else's skin for a while"—he made a face—"that sounds terrible, but I . . ."

She waited.

"Stepping into someone else's life, trying it on for a while, figuring out all of the little pieces that go into making a person react the way they do. Why they say things, or how they speak, or what becomes that critical thing for them to drag their heels on." His eyes lit up. "Because everyone is different, you know? My line in the sand might be something as simple and stupid as having a proper cup of coffee in the morning, maybe yours is organization and keeping all of your ducks in a line, maybe my agent's is getting as much money as possible so he's never at risk of living again like how he grew up. And acting gave me the space to explore all of that, to understand it."

"But you haven't felt that way lately?"

"No."

"Is it—" She stopped, trying to phrase the question in her mind differently, because she was wondering if the trauma of what was done to his sister had taken away his enjoyment for his craft.

If perhaps he blamed himself for being away or somehow thought his fame had made her a target.

"About my sister?" he asked as she was struggling with wording.

Shan nodded.

"I'm sure it is in some way." He sighed. "I'm sure it is in a *lot* of ways. She was at a party for an actor friend of mine, took the rapist she met there up on his offer to drive her home. If I wasn't doing what I was doing, she would have never been at that party at all."

"And she thought it was safe because the host was your friend."

He didn't say anything for a long time. "I should have been there," he said. "I was supposed to be. But I'd just gotten in from a long shoot, and I was tired—" He broke off, shoved a hand through his hair.

"You blame yourself," she said, confirming her earlier thought.

"How can I not?" he asked. "I didn't go, and that happened to her. I should have sent her in a car, should have been there in the first place—" He broke off, hands fisting on his thighs.

"Trauma is an odd thing."

His gaze flicked to hers.

"My mother was an addict. Opioids. OxyContin. Percocet. Vicodin." She sighed. "Then heroin. And eventually, what would be her downfall, fentanyl."

"Shannon." The tension left him, and he scooted closer, slipped an arm around her shoulders. "Shit. I'm sorry."

"No," she said. "I didn't bring it up to try to out-trauma you. I . . . well, my point is that my mom died when I was twelve. OD'd. I found her after school and called 9-1-1 and there was nothing they could do. She was gone." Shannon inhaled and exhaled slowly, putting that old pain back into its box, carefully locking it. "I went to live with my dad at that point. An arrangement he wasn't too thrilled about, especially when he'd—direct quote here—dodged a bullet with my mom. He didn't want another female of *her* blood in his life."

"That's—"

"Horrible. Terrible." She nodded as he slid his hand up and down her back. "All the -ble's," she said, going for a weak joke. "It *was*. I'd spent a long time taking care of her, and then I went to my dad's and I spent the rest of my childhood trying to make him proud of me." Her eyes slid shut. "Newsflash. It didn't work."

"Asshole."

"In a lot of ways," Shan said, with a broken laugh. "I agree with you. But the trauma of dealing with my mom brought that side out in him. Granted, not all of it, because he wasn't a gem in ways that were many and copious, but living with an addict affects people differently, trauma affects people in strange and painful ways. My dad did his thing. I did mine. We were both sliced to pieces inside."

"Except, family is supposed to help you heal those hurt pieces."

"My dad wasn't capable of that."

Finn sighed and sat back. "That's bullshit. That's *not* what a good parent does."

"You're right."

"Then how can you talk so calmly about it?"

"He couldn't be what I needed."

"That's—"

"The painful truth," she said. "Right around the time I found out that Brian was cheating, I realized how much I'd shrunk myself down in order to try to be this perfect person for him, just liked I tried to do for my dad. I'm still working on it, still find myself fighting the urge to bend and transform myself into what people want from me."

"Blue Eyes."

"I'm different now. I *promised* myself it would be different." She touched his cheek, ignoring the pity in his tone. "It's a promise I'm scared I won't be able to keep."

"You will."

She bit her lip. "I hope so." She wrinkled her nose. "Did you know that I didn't even want to be a teacher?" she said. "I became one because my grandmother taught for years and I thought my dad would take pride in it."

"Did he?"

"I don't know." She shrugged. "But he didn't express any pride, and I found myself in a career I didn't love because I tried to live for someone else."

"And do you love it now?" he asked. "Or would you want to make a change?"

Did she?

"There are parts I do love," she said. "And there are parts that are the worst, but any job is like that, right? It's never going to be one hundred rainbows and unicorns all the time."

He nodded. "That's true."

"So, now I've redirected the conversation completely back to me," she said. "I was trying to say that just because the trauma didn't happen to you, doesn't mean you weren't affected." She put her hand up. "And that's not to discount your sister and her trauma because that's what's most important. It's just this kind of stuff . . . isn't singular, you know? A rock being tossed into a lake creates ripples, and those ripples flow and move over objects in their path, and they can be changed." She blew out a breath. "I'm sorry, I'm rambling, and that probably doesn't make sense."

"You're wrong."

Her gut sank. "I—"

"You're not rambling," he said, leaning forward again and cupping her cheek. "Once again, I'm just amazed by your ability to take something so tangled and misshapen in my mind and put it into words."

"Well, if the words are working, then I'll take it." She smiled.

He bent to brush his mouth across hers. "They're working." Another brush. "Also, you're amazing." He nipped her bottom lip. "I hope you'll at least take that."

"Finn."

He ran his fingers along her jaw. "It's true, Blue Eyes."

Her heart swelled, warmth spreading out and filling her from head to toe. Just being next to Finn, being held and touched by him was wonderful. And being able to talk to him about things both important and not made it even better.

"I like you, Finn Stoneman."

"Well, that's a good thing, because I like *you*, Shannon Torres."

More warmth. More . . . heat.

Propelling her into confidence, into doing something she'd never had the courage to do before.

She made the first move.

Leaning forward, she closed the distance between their mouths and put every single bit of warmth and heat and *like* for this man into that kiss.

His tongue slipped between her lips, rubbing against hers,

sending sparks of need throughout her body as his arms wrapped tightly around her, and they kissed and kissed and *kissed.* Eventually, they broke apart, chests heaving, her pulse pounding in her ears. She rested her forehead against his, breaths mingling, the space between her thighs wet and aching. Finn's honey eyes had deepened to amber, and the sight of them staring hotly at her made her desire ramp up even further.

But Rylie was down the hall.

And . . . she wasn't ready.

So, she shifted in his embrace and reached for the remote. "I like you, Finn Stoneman, but I think I like you even more with those extra thirty pounds of muscle."

He grinned, tucked her against his chest, and stole the remote.

"Then I guess I'd better take advantage of that six months without carbs in any way I can."

He hit play, and they watched the end of the movie cuddled together.

For the record, Finn might not think the film would change lives, but he was absolutely wrong.

Because it had already changed hers.

———

"I'm sorry, Beatrice," Shannon said into her cell a few days later. "But I can't cover your club tomorrow"—like she always did. Shan swore she might as well be the leader for how often she ran the sessions—"Rylie has an important dance class that she can't miss, and I promised her teacher that I would video the girls."

A beat, probably because Shannon wanting to please everyone in her world hadn't just begun and ended with the men in her life.

She bent over backward for *everyone* and to her own detriment.

Well, that had ended.

"Can't someone else film?" Beatrice asked.

"Sorry, no," Shannon replied.

"But—"

"I need to go," she said, pausing only to say a quick goodbye before pocketing her cell. She smiled as she walked toward the railing of the deck, leaning back against it, feeling the cool, salt-tinged air coat her skin, listening to the crash of the waves. Yeah, it felt good to have a backbone.

Good enough that she didn't care if Beatrice was mad and gave her the silent treatment. Good enough that she thought she could keep standing up for herself, keep growing into a person that Rylie would be proud of one day.

A person *she* could be proud of.

Her.

Yes, for once she was as important to herself as the rest of the people in her universe.

Progress.

Small progress.

But she'd take it, just like she'd continue taking these baby steps moving forward.

Brian hadn't shown up.

Again.

Fucking hell.

And now Rylie was playing on the deck, having avoided the sand because Brian didn't like it in his car, and as the hours went on, her daughter's face got sadder and sadder.

"Shit," she muttered, putting her book aside and picking up her cell.

She'd thought they were done with this.

She'd thought that with their lives separated that Brian would be able to put away the anger he'd been fostering toward her and focus on the innocent being they'd created together.

Instead . . . he didn't show up.

"I'll be right back, honey," she said, forcing herself to modulate her tone.

"Okay," Rylie said.

And it was the just *said* part that was the problem. Because Ry didn't talk at a normal volume. She yelled and cheered, filled every word with excitement.

Except . . . with Brian.

Ugh.

Because she'd learned that behavior from Shannon.

Well, no more.

So, instead of going around the corner like she always did, instead of quietly talking in the corner, listening to Brian berate her while trying to get a word in edgewise, she sucked in a deep breath, forced herself to sit back into her chair, and dialed her ex's phone number.

Ring-ring. Ring-ring. Ring-ring.

Voicemail.

Asshole.

She took another breath, listened through Brian's voice telling her to leave a message. Then after the beep, she said, "You were supposed to be here three hours ago to take your daughter for the night. You missed out on spending time with our wonderful girl. Again. She's awesome and strong and sweet and kind and she wants to spend time with her dad." Another breath. "Not have her heart broken because you can't be bothered to show up. Again." Shan's eyes slid closed. "I'm calling only to tell you that this will not happen again because I'm having Alberto renegotiate our custody agreement, so it *never* happens again."

Then she hung up.

Phone on the table, book in her hand, deep breath to concentrate on the words.

This was fine. She could do this.

"Mom?"

"Yeah, honey?"

"You sounded mad."

Shannon's throat burned. "I am mad, Rylie boo."

"At me?"

She pushed out of her seat, hurried over to her daughter. "No, baby. Not at you at all. I love you so much." She cupped Ry's cheek. "I'm mad that you were waiting. I'm mad that you missed out on a fun time. But I'm not mad at you. I love you."

Ry nodded, but her expression didn't clear.

Fuck.

Shannon slipped her arm around her. "It's okay to be sad."

"I know."

"But it's also okay to find stuff that makes us happy."

Ry tilted her head up, eyes coming to Shannon's. "What makes you happy?"

"You." Her daughter made a face. "And ice cream."

"Ice cream?"

She nodded, lips tugging up at the edges. "Yup."

"Can we get some?"

Another nod. "Yeah, baby. We sure can." She stood. "Let's go get our jackets on and get root beer floats from the diner, okay?"

Ry grinned. "Root beer floats? Really?"

"*Really* really."

And maybe she was giving her daughter poor coping skills

or putting an improper emphasis on food and her daughter's relationship with it. But know what? The root beer floats at the diner were the best. They *did* make her feel better and . . .

Did she really need to worry about and measure out every single thing she did?

Could she just relax about the expectations?

Could she and Ry just be? Just live and not stress over everything?

A year ago she would have said no.

Today, she knew that if her life and her daughter's was going to be a happy one, then she'd have to.

But that was okay because she *wanted* to.

"Root beer floats!" Ry shouted, running for the house, presumably for her jacket.

"Root beer floats?" a masculine voice asked, sending heat arrowing down between Shannon's thighs. She spun, saw Finn there. "Hey, Blue Eyes," he said. "Everything okay?"

"Yup," she told him. "Ry and I are going to get root beer floats at the diner."

"Spoiling your dinner?"

A shrug. "Probably." Then she did something that fit right in with her promise to worry less, to live more, to *be* more for herself and her daughter. She grinned up at Finn and asked, "Want to have your world rocked again?"

He stepped closer, voice going husky. "What do you have in mind?"

Wobbling knees. A skipping pulse. The way those intense honey eyes fixed on hers.

God, she wanted to kiss him again.

Their mouths were an inch apart. Hot breath on her lips, a slightly calloused palm on her cheek. "I—"

"Root beer floats!" Rylie yelled, tearing out of the house, the door slamming behind her.

Finn straightened, fingers sliding from her cheek. "So close."

She nibbled at the corner of her mouth. "So far." A beat. "For the record, the floats will rock your world, too."

"Hmm."

Shan started to turn for the front door, but Finn caught her arm, tugged her back around to face him.

"What—"

He kissed her, one brief firm press of his mouth to hers that had her knees going weak. Then he released her, nudged her toward the door, saying, "Get a jacket, wind's picking up."

"Are you coming with us, Mr. Finn?" she heard Ry call, while grabbing her jacket from the hook in the hallway.

"Is that okay with you, Ms Rylie?" Finn asked.

Ry's "Yup!" was punctuated with pounding footsteps across the deck and had Shannon grinning. "Root beer floats are the best!"

Yeah, this less worrying, more living thing was pretty great.

FOURTEEN
RESOLUTION ON THE DOTTED LINE

Finn

"AND THAT'S the final signature right there," the mid-twenties-something notary said, pointing at one last line.

Finn scrawled his name on the line, took his copy of the paperwork, and then slipped out the door and onto the sidewalk.

He was one town over.

His assistant had called that morning to say he'd found a house and the deal for it was done—easy, Finn supposed when he'd offered the sellers all cash, over asking price, and to take the property as is. It was ocean-front with an identical layout to the cottage he was staying in, and the address told him it wasn't far from it either.

He'd have to wait until the payment processed and the keys were turned over, but that shouldn't take long.

Then he'd have his home base here.

Then he could keep spending time with Shannon.

It had been two weeks since they'd watched the movie together, and he'd seen her and Rylie every day—sometimes for just a cup of coffee and the walk to school, twice more he'd brought her takeout for dinner, and once he'd brought her lunch at school.

All of that had given him even more proof for why he loved this town.

Not one picture of him had appeared in any newspaper or social media post, not even the selfie he'd taken with the teenager more than a month before.

So yeah, even if Shannon and Rylie weren't here, Stoneybrook would be high on his list of places to have a house.

He slid into his car, dropped the papers into the back seat, and turned on the ignition. Privacy, a beautiful woman, an awesome little girl who was energetic and sweet and funny.

He'd bought houses sight unseen multiple times in the past.

This was the first time he'd known with one hundred percent certainty that he would be thrilled about the purchase.

Because Shannon.

Because Rylie.

Yeah, he couldn't wait to set up a home here.

SHE CAME to his deck that night, a mug in her hand, fluffy pajamas on her legs, and an oversized hoodie covering her curves. "Do you mind company?" she asked, gesturing to the laptop open in front of him.

"No," he said. "I was just reading through a project."

"A new film?"

"T.V. actually," he told her. "Or well, for a streaming platform."

She sank into the chair next to him. "That seems out of the ordinary for you."

A shrug. "I haven't done it before, but I've been . . ." He trailed off.

"What?" she asked, resting the mug down on the table and covering his hand with hers. "What is it?"

"Hollywood problems," he said. "More selfish need to feed my soul, more not finding anywhere where *I* fit in." He closed his laptop and sighed. "And more of me being totally aware of how ridiculous that sounds being a straight, white man."

She squeezed his hand. "Well, I will say I agree that your category of story has been told more than most." A soft smile. "But I don't think it's wrong to search for different ways to tell that story, different pieces of yourself you haven't had the chance to explore yet."

"How do you always have the words?" he asked.

She chuckled. "Well, if you find the story for a single mom with a jerky ex who looks like me and not some blond, skinny Hollywood type, let it be known, I'll buy the first ticket."

He tucked a strand of hair behind her ear. "You've got a deal." A beat. "Cute jammies, by the way."

A snort. "Really?"

"They're adorable." He grinned. "I've always loved sheep."

Those pretty blue eyes danced with laughter. "You can't help but be charming, can you?"

"It's a gift."

She took a sip from her mug.

"Coffee this late at night?"

"No." She shook her head. "Hot chocolate." She extended the cup. "Want some?"

He wanted something, and it wasn't hot chocolate. His mouth watered with the desire, the *need* to kiss her, to touch her again. "No, thanks."

She shrugged, leaned forward to place the mug on the table again.

They sat in silence for several long moments before Shan turned back to face him again, studying him closely, searching his eyes, the heavy weight of her stare almost tangible as it traced over him.

"What is it?"

The corners of her mouth tipped up. "I just realized why I came over here tonight."

Finn tilted his head to the side. "Was it not for my charming personality?"

That mouth curving further. "No, honey. I came over here because I wanted to kiss you again."

Lightning through his veins.

He sat up straight, the statement pretty much the last one he'd expected to come off her tongue. "What—?"

"Is that okay?" she asked, standing up and spinning to face him, then sitting back down, only this time astride his thighs. "Is *this* okay? I've been promising myself I'd do less worrying, that I'd start living and feeling and just . . . going for it." Her expression became tinged with shy. "Is that—well, I mean . . . is that—"

His words wouldn't come, at least until the moment she faltered, the moment uncertainty crept into her face.

Then Finn found himself unfrozen.

"Yeah, Blue Eyes," he said, sliding one hand behind her head, dropping the other to her waist and tugging her close. "That's more than okay."

He kissed her.

And later, when he'd walked her to her front door, pressed a gentle kiss to swollen and slightly-reddened lips, he was beyond grateful that he'd bought the house.

Beyond. Grateful.

The phone call came when he was already in bed that night a few days later, having missed Rylie and Shannon for dinner because of his trip to the next town and because they'd both been busy with Back to School Night.

Now it was almost eleven, he'd been tucked into bed with a script open on his computer, and Shan had said she and Rylie would come over for breakfast in the morning, since it was Saturday.

He was going to make French toast.

With chocolate sauce—per Ry's suggestion.

Grinning and lost in the memory of her fist-pump upon sight of Lizzy, as they'd all walked to school that morning, Finn jumped when his phone buzzed again. He set his laptop to the side, picked up his cell, glanced at the screen . . . and felt his heart seize.

Lexy.

His sister.

His *younger* sister. Who'd told him to go. Who—

Buzz. Buzz.

Whose call he was going to miss if he didn't pick up the *damn* phone.

Scrambling, he swiped his finger across the screen. "Lex?"

"Finn." A shaky breath. "I'm here."

"Here, *where?*"

"On your porch."

He sat bolt upright in bed, heart clenching again. "On my porch," he repeated. "In Stoneybrook?"

"Y-yes."

The cell hit the bed the same moment his feet hit the hardwood floor. Then he took off for the front door, footsteps pounding down the hall, and he hauled ass for the person he could see silhouetted by the overhead lights through the window in the white wood.

He reached for the knob, wrenched open the door.

"Lex."

"Finn," she said, her expression unreadable.

He opened his arms.

She took a faltering step forward and fell into them.

Then she was crying.

Then Finn was crying as he tugged her inside, leading her over to the couch. All the while, Lexy's tears didn't stop, great wrenching sobs that soaked through the T-shirt he wore, heart-breaking pain that sliced through him with each hiccupping breath that passed through her lungs.

His own eyes were burning, leaking hot tears down his cheeks, but he did the only thing he could.

Held on to his sister as they both cried.

For everything that had happened. For everything that had changed.

For everything that had been violated and lost.

He didn't even realize he'd been repeating, "I'm sorry" over and over again until she pushed off his chest, cupped his face in her palms and said, "It's not your fault."

"Lex," he began, voice rough. "I—"

She jostled his face. "It's. Not. Your. Fault," she repeated. "Nothing that happened that night was your fault or my fault. It was *his* fault. *He* was wrong. *He* violated me and took what wasn't freely given. But that's not on you or me."

He covered her palms with his fingers, gently peeling her hands from his face. "Lex, you shouldn't be trying to make me feel better. You should be concentrating on you."

"I did concentrate on me," she said. "I've spent the last months concentrating on me, on my healing, on processing what happened, what was done to me."

"You should keep doing that," he said. "Not fly out here and—"

"I told you to go."

He winced.

She turned her hands over in his, squeezed his fingers lightly. "I told you to go because every time I looked over the dinner table, seeing you there as the media storm grew, watching you in agony week after week after week, I just . . . I couldn't take it."

He swallowed hard. "I'm sorry."

"Finn."

His eyes flicked back to hers.

"I was never mad at you about the interview, about how it came out."

"I shouldn't have—" He shook his head, sat back. "I violated your privacy and—"

"The only one who violated *anything* was my rapist."

"I—"

"And further that I was proud of you for standing up for that girl, for calling out that sleazeball of an anchor. *That* was the right thing to do." A ghost of a smile. "Maybe I would have liked some warning . . . but—"

He shook his head. "Lexy, I get what you're doing, but—"

"I *was* angry at you."

His lungs froze.

"I was furious. I hated that you were famous enough to get me an invite to that party, that you didn't come and protect me. I was hurt and shattered inside, and *I was so fucking mad* at you."

"You should be."

"No, Finn," she said. "The person I should be furious at is my rapist."

"I—" What could he say? Because she was right, but that also didn't excuse his role. If he'd just been there, then things would be different.

"Guilt train."

His brows dragged together. "What?"

"You're all aboard the guilt train, and you don't want to get off," she said. "You stay on it, you keep beating yourself up, thinking you deserve this punishment, but in reality, you're punishing me."

"Lex."

"Because if you stop living, if you keep hurting yourself"— she sniffed—"then you need to know that you're hurting me, too."

He tugged her into his arms. "Lex."

"He hurt us enough," she murmured. "Let's not allow him to keep doing it."

Finn held her tight. Partly in wonder because how had his sister gotten so big and grown-up when he'd had to help her tie her shoes all the way up to fifth grade? Partly because he felt so lucky that she was there and safe and had survived the awful thing that was done to her. "You were right to tell me to go."

"Hey—"

He loosened his arms, leaned back to meet her eyes. "You needed space to heal, not me freaking out and making it worse."

"That's not what I came to say."

"I know," he said. "But it's what I need to say. I was never hurt because you told me to go. I got it, and you were right. I needed out of town, just as much as you needed me gone." He twisted, leaned back so his shoulder rested against the cushions and he faced her. "The media was relentless. Every time they hounded you, I felt worse. And, let's face it, they were there for me. When I left, things got better." A beat. "For both of us."

Her head tilted to the side. "They haven't found you here?"

"No." He shrugged. "This town is great. I haven't had a single person hound me, no stories of my exploits on the gossip sites. It's so great that I bought a place."

Lex smiled. "Of course, you did."

"Wait until you see it in the daylight," he told her. "The sunrise is gorgeous."

"I feel silly for waiting to drive over until this late."

"Where were you?"

"Sitting at a diner, reading a paperback. My flight got in, and I drove to Stoneybrook a few hours ago. Oh!" She pushed off the couch, went to the front door, and grabbed a small backpack that she must have dropped on his deck. "I can't believe I left this out here—" She reached inside, tugged out a book, and extended it toward him. "But anyway. I think this needs to be your next project."

Her yawn punctuated the paperback hitting his palm.

"Hit the hay," he told her, nudging her in the direction of his bedroom. There was only one in his cottage, the second bedroom having been made into an office.

But he'd be fine on the couch for a night.

"I'm all right"—another yawn—"I want to catch up with you—"

He snagged her backpack and pushed in front of her, bringing it into the bedroom and setting it on the chair just inside the door. "You're exhausted from being on a plane all day. Get some sleep, and we can catch up tomorrow."

No more arguments.

She just nodded and unzipped the large compartment of her backpack and extracted some pajamas. "Okay." Another yawn.

"Bathroom's through there. There's a spare toothbrush under the sink."

"Okay," she said again. "Can I borrow a T-shirt?"

Finn grabbed one out of his dresser and tossed it to her, then turned to pull a blanket out of the closet, a pillow and his laptop and cell off the bed as she disappeared into the bathroom to change, then got himself settled on the couch.

Lex appeared a few minutes later, clad in his shirt and fluffy penguin pajama bottoms, and looking about twelve years old.

"Love you, middle bro," she said, giving him a hug.

"Love you, littlest sis."

She grinned.

"Sleep tight," he told her and watched as she went back down the hall and closed the door to the bedroom. He knew she'd be out in approximately ten seconds, because that was her superpower: give Lex a semi-horizontal surface and a modicum of tiredness and the girl could *sleep*.

He'd always been so jealous of her on road trips, both of them crowded into the back of the minivan with their siblings, Lex sleeping through the bickering as the miles slipped by.

Tonight, just like then, he knew it would be nearly impossible to fall asleep.

He had too much to think about.

Too much to process.

But somewhere around the time the sun began to rise, his eyes were finally heavy enough to slide shut.

And, what felt like mere moments later, they opened back up to chaos.

Complete and utter chaos.

FIFTEEN
THE OTHER WOMAN

Shannon

SHE KNOCKED on the front door, frowning at the quiet of the house.

Rylie was wriggling next to her, almost vibrating herself out of her skin—if such a thing were even possible, her daughter would manage to get that jumping, dancing skeleton right out of her body and prance along the porch.

But those fictional dancing bones couldn't answer the door.

She knocked one more time, waited a few more minutes.

"Why isn't Mr. Finn answering, Mom?"

"He's probably sleeping, honey." She tugged the end of Ry's ponytail. "Let's go back to our house and make French toast. When we're done, we'll come back over and knock again."

Ry made a face. "Okay," she muttered.

"He probably just stayed up too late. Remember how hard it was to get up that time you tried not to go to sleep?"

Her daughter considered that. "Yeah, I remember."

"So, we'll make our French toast extra good, in case Finn is grumpy when we come back and knock again."

"With extra powdered sugar?"

"Yup." She started to turn. "And maybe even with bananas."

"Bananas!"

She grinned. "Let's go—"

The door opened.

A beautiful blond woman stood there, one hand on the wooden frame, the other on the knob. "Can I help you?"

She was wearing a T-shirt of Finn's.

Shannon knew because she remembered with crystal clarity the last time he'd worn it. Standing on her deck. Well, leaning against the railing of her deck, the disappearing sunlight emphasizing the strong lines of his jaw and cheekbones, wind ruffling his hair. She'd just come back from checking on Rylie inside, making sure she was settling down for bed, then had emerged to the sight of a Greek god.

Frozen in place.

Emerald green shirt that made his eyes look almost other-worldly.

Then he'd smiled at her.

And she'd gone, a fish to bait, a mouse to a trap, recognizing the danger but still drawn forward, unbidden, unable to stop herself.

One step. Another. *Another.*

When she'd gotten close enough, he'd reached out, snaked an arm around her waist, pulled her against his chest, and he'd kissed her.

Kissed her until her head spun.

Kissed her until she forgot about the danger.

Kissed her until she believed the danger hadn't existed in the first place.

And she'd spent the last month in a bubble, a safely-padded cocoon where it had just been this wonderful, lovely man with her and Rylie. Walking to school, sharing meals, stealing kisses.

New and exciting, comfortable and . . . normal.

But in all of that newness and comfort and *normal*, she'd forgotten that he was the biggest actor in the world. That while the people of Stoneybrook might not be impressed by fame, while they were used to seeing celebrities, to seeing people like Pepper and Finn as, well, just *people*, Finn *wasn't* normal.

This was the real world.

This was Hollywood.

And, she couldn't stop the small, insidious voice in her head telling her this is what men who were interested in her did. They turned to other women.

"We want to see Mr. Finn!" Ry said.

Well, shouted because Ry never just talked.

But that burst of words was enough to get Shannon moving. It didn't matter that Finn had a woman in his house. It didn't matter that she'd thought they were building . . . whatever it was she'd thought they'd been building.

Because clearly, she was wrong.

Yet, it didn't matter.

It wouldn't break her, she wouldn't fall to pieces. She had a job and a place to live and a daughter who was awesome.

So, fuck him.

Fuck men.

Fuck letting herself be broken again and again and again.

"Come on, Ry," she said. "We'll see Mr. Finn later." Where she'd tell him to go *fuck* himself because she was done with the opposite sex and all of their bullshit.

"Wait!" the woman said. "I—"

"I *want* to see Mr. Finn!"

Shan gaped for a second. Rylie never used that tone. *Never.* For one, she didn't tolerate being talked to in that way. For another, her daughter might be loud, but she was perpetually happy.

Of course, her gaping had a negative effect.

One that meant Ry was able to use those few seconds to ramp up higher, to spiral further. By the time Shan closed her mouth and pulled back into herself, her daughter's typically adorable face had clouded with fury.

"I. Want. To. See. Finn!" she yelled.

"Rylie Marie Torres," Shannon snapped, using her combined powers of Mom Voice and Teacher Voice. "You will not speak like that."

Rylie's mouth closed with an audible *click*.

"I'm sorry to interrupt," Shannon said, forcing herself to look back at the beautiful woman in the doorway. "We'll be going now."

"Wait—"

Shannon didn't wait.

She'd seen enough, and now it was time to return to her regularly scheduled life. She'd gotten to kiss a movie star, that should be enough for her to hold on to at this time, right?

It was more than she'd ever imagined, that was for sure.

She took Rylie's hand, started to leave Finn's deck.

"No!" Ry yanked herself free. "No!" She darted for the house. "Finn. *Finn!*"

The woman in the doorway was shocked, her mouth dropping open, no doubt because a young child was hurtling toward her. But then she was pushed aside, and Finn emerged from inside the house, shirtless and looking rumpled, his eyes sleepy, his hair mussed.

Rylie hurtled toward him, throwing her arms around his waist and knocking him back a step.

His arms went around her, but his eyes stayed up, coming first to Shannon's then to the woman next to him.

Regret on his face.

Fuck, that hurt.

But she kept her spine stiff, her chin lifted. This would be fine. She wouldn't break. She—

"Shannon," he said carefully. "This is my sister, Lexy."

Hot then cold washed over her. Embarrassment crippled her, froze her in place, made bile burn the back of her throat.

His sister.

That was good, right? A logical, reasonable explanation for a strange woman in his house in the morning. But also . . . it undercut exactly how *not* ready for this she was. Her first thought had been Finn was cheating, and they weren't even in an exclusive relationship—or they hadn't talked about it, anyway.

Because it all came down to this.

Her believing deep down that she wasn't worthy or good enough, and *dammit* she wanted to believe she was good enough, wanted it so fucking badly.

Why couldn't she believe it?

What was wrong with her that she couldn't?

Her eyes burned and she turned away, gaze on the ocean but not taking in the waves. She held the tears but didn't want anyone to see how close to the edge she was. "Come on, Ry, we need to go."

"No."

More unexpected attitude. More teenage-esque tone. More . . . things to deal with later.

She heard the soft rumble of Finn's voice then slow footsteps trailing across the deck toward her. Thank God, Rylie wasn't going to require her to yank her away from Finn. She couldn't handle that.

"Trauma."

A male voice.

"It ripples outward and engulfs everything in its path."

Her breath shuddered out. "Finn, I can't—"

"Lexy took Rylie inside. They're starting the French toast." He slipped his fingers around her arm, gently turned her to face him. "You and I are going to talk about whatever it is that just went through your mind."

"It's nothing." She forced a smile.

"It's definitely something," he muttered, caging her in against the railing, his body flush against hers, making heat cascade over her body again, only this time it wasn't due to embarrassment. He dropped his head, ran his jaw along hers. "Because you're doing that sad smile again, and I fucking hate that sad smile." He nipped, and she jumped. "Also, I'm pretty sure I know why you've got sad written all over you, and it fucking pisses me off."

"Finn."

"Shannon."

She sighed. "I can't do this."

"I'm not your ex-husband."

"Finn."

"Shannon," he repeated, taking them right down the same pattern.

"We don't make sense."

"I stopped worrying about things making sense the first time I saw you, Blue Eyes. You're special. You're mine," he said, and her heart skipped a beat. "I've been trying to go slow because you're not officially divorced and need time to heal, because you've been hurt too many times, because you've got Rylie and need to make sure she's good. But let me make this crystal clear for you. You're. Mine."

Her head dropped to his shoulder. "Finn."

He wove his fingers into her hair, held her there. "Shannon." She sighed.

He pressed a kiss to the top of her head. "Come inside. Let's make breakfast. I want you to meet my sister."

"She probably thinks I'm a lunatic."

"She took one look at me and knew you're more important to me than any other woman has ever been."

Shannon's breath caught, and she leaned back to meet his gaze, the intensity in those honey-colored eyes making her heart skip a beat. "Finn," she murmured, blurting his name like an idiot. Again.

"Shannon." He grinned.

"I don't think—"

"Good. *Stop* thinking. Just come alongside me on the feeling thing, okay?"

She nibbled at the corner of her mouth, wanting to go alongside with him more than anything, but also . . . fucking terrified what would happen if she did.

He didn't press, just waited as she ran through all the possibilities and ways things could end in disaster through her mind. There were a lot of freaking ways this could all go wrong—the media and the frightening multitude of ways they may infiltrate her and Ry's life, Finn being away on films and being tempted by women much more beautiful than her, falling in love with him only to find out he'd not fallen alongside, or worse, to risk finding out one day that he might fall out of love, like Brian had.

But . . . were any of those scenarios scarier than the possibility of *never* seeing where this might lead?

Of living her whole life knowing she'd had a chance at something that made her feel all of these big things and not having found the courage to reach out and grasp on to it? To jump in and live?

What would she miss out on?

What kind of example would she be setting for her daughter?

Too much. And the wrong one.

She released a shuddering breath. "I'm putting my heart into your hands," she said.

"Mine is already in yours." He tucked a strand of hair behind her ear. "I've shared more with you than anyone on the planet, Blue Eyes. I've trusted you with *everything* when I'm in a position where that can be a very dangerous thing." He cupped the side of her neck. "I've done that because this connection between us is different, is more than anything I could have hoped for. I'm falling in love with you, Shannon Torres, and I'm going to do everything in my power to not fuck it up."

Was it hot in here?

Out here?

Either way, his words made her knees weak, equal parts incredible and terrifying, and Finn knew that because he tugged her close, held her tight. "See? This is why I've been moving slow."

She chuckled, leaning heavily against him. "I think it's so scary because if I look at all the pieces, they don't seem to fit. I'm not even divorced yet! But then I spend time with you, I see you with Rylie . . . and it's just everything I've ever wanted and everything I've been terrified to hope for." She swallowed hard. "Because once upon a time, I thought my future was figured out."

"And he hurt you."

She nodded. "You know what's scarier, though?"

A shake of his head.

"Imagining how sad and pathetic the rest of my life would be, knowing I had a chance to see where things went with us but was too terrified to actually take the leap." She touched his cheek. "I'm falling for you, too."

He released a breath, relief spreading over his features, softening them. "Come out to dinner with me tonight. Let's go on a real date."

"Ry—"

"I'll bribe my sister into watching her." He rested his forehead against hers. "Or Pepper."

"I—"

"A real date, Blue Eyes. You and me and some wine. Maybe a nice dress and heels. I'll wear a suit and tie."

Mmm. Finn in a suit and tie. She'd love to hold on to that scrap of silk, use it to tug him closer until his lips settled onto hers.

"What just went through your mind?" he asked, voice husky.

She told him.

He grinned. "Does that mean you'll go on a date with me?"

"Yes." Shannon nodded, lifting up on tiptoe to brush her mouth over hers.

As these things tended to happen, a simple brush turned into much more. Her lips parted, his tongue slid inside her mouth, and desire rippled down her spine. She moaned, pressed closer, loving that his chest rumbled against hers in response, loving that this man could kiss her well enough to make her head spin.

Eventually, though, he pulled back, cupping her cheek lightly with one hand. "I'll wear a tie if you bring the heels."

Shannon's heart bubbled up with joy. "Deal."

Then he laced their fingers together and led her into the cottage to meet his sister . . . which turned out to be less meeting and more rescuing her from Rylie's love of powdered sugar.

Just saying, Shannon couldn't deny that it also made the French toast taste better than ever.

Or maybe, that was just the company.

SIXTEEN
FEELS LIKE THE FIRST TIME

Finn

HE WAS SITTING across the table from a beautiful woman, and he couldn't taste his food.

Not because it wasn't delicious.

But because it just didn't matter.

Not when he was sitting across from Shannon.

They'd spent most of their meal bantering like always, nibbling at their entrees, drinking two bottles of wine, and sharing a piece of chocolate cake between them. But the consumption of food and drink wasn't in the forefront of his mind, not in the least.

What dominated was the heat between them.

Boiling up from beneath the surface, inundating the space between them, sparking whenever their eyes met, or their legs accidentally brushed under the table . . . or whenever Shan leaned forward or smiled or laughed or *breathed*.

He wanted this woman.

And her gaze was saying she wanted him right back.

But Finn wasn't going to have her—or not that night anyway. He'd pressed her that morning, had seen her fear, and while he knew she'd pushed past that, he also knew that she wasn't impervious to the memories or completely free from what had happened to her.

So, sticking with slow and steady.

Rylie was with Lexy at Shannon's house, no surprise that the two had hit it off. Finn had a pre-release copy of a new kid's film coming out in a couple of weeks, so Ry and Lex were having a girl's movie night complete with sundaes and mani/pedis, and once Shannon had been convinced the babysitting would not be an inconvenience to Lexy, she'd allowed Finn to make dinner reservations and had hit the grocery store for supplies.

When they'd left the girls a few hours earlier, Lexy and Ry had been in their pajamas already, mani/pedi supplies laid out on the glass table.

Now, he was pleasantly full, somehow still surprised to find that had happened, considering he hadn't really tasted anything that had crossed his lips, and he was ready to have Shan to himself.

"Let's take a walk on the beach," he said.

She looked up at him from under her lashes. "I'd have to lose the heels."

He shrugged. "You can always put them back on later."

"That'd be a crime to my toes."

"Oh, shit. Are they uncomfortable?"

A shrug. "I think the correct question is, are heels *ever* comfortable? And the answer to that question is no"—a grin, no trace of sad, and Finn knew in that moment he wasn't falling for her, he'd been gone for Shannon a long time ago—"but we get used to it."

"Well," he said, reaching for the little leather folder that held the bill. "We can do the walk, but they're not going back on. Not if it's going to hurt you."

"And how am I going to get home?"

"I'll carry you." He flipped open the cover and frowned.

Shannon flipped it closed. "I got it earlier when you went to the bathroom."

"What?"

She stood, and instinctively Finn followed suit. "You got what?" he asked, helping her with her coat, though it was a shame to cover up that luscious body clad in the black silk dress that had been driving him crazy all night.

"I got the bill."

"*What?*"

She grinned, patted him on the cheek. "Let's go on that walk now."

"Shannon—"

She strode to the front door of the restaurant, hips swaying, making his cock twitch, fists clench with the urge to catch up to her, tug her back against him and show her exactly what those heels and her dress and that *fucking* incredible strut did to him.

Instead, he hurried to catch up, to move beyond her, and open the front door.

That got him a heated smile, a brush of her body against his as she moved through.

He followed her, slipping an arm around her waist. "Blue Eyes—"

"Is this about the bill?" She melted against him, one hand coming up to rest on his chest. "Or the fact that all night I've been imagining you clearing the food from our table with one arm and spreading me on the table and eating *me* instead?" A beat, her lips finding his ear. "And that I think you've been doing the same."

Well, he damn sure was *now*.

"Shan."

"Let's walk back to your place," she said.

He didn't stop her when she led them down the path toward the beach one block over, helped her when she paused and lifted one foot then the other to slip off her shoes. When they were dangling from her fingertips, she turned to him and pressed her lips to his.

Heat exploded.

He tugged her against him, banded his arms tightly around her, and kissed her until he had forgotten about the table and instead wanted to spread her out on the sand and—

She broke away, lips swollen, breaths coming in rapid gusts.

His weren't any steadier. "You shouldn't have paid for dinner," he said, tugging her against his side and turning them in the direction of his house.

She glanced up at him, amusement dancing across her face. "You gave me a kiss like that, and you're worried about the bill."

"I was taking you out, Blue Eyes." He ran a finger down her nose. "It was supposed to be *my* treat."

"And when was the last time someone treated you?" she murmured.

His retort caught in the back of his throat because . . . he couldn't remember.

"Yeah," she said. "That's why." She nudged him with her shoulder as they came to his deck, but instead of stopping there and sitting in one of the chairs, as had become their routine for most nights they'd spent together, she bypassed the furniture and went to his front door.

He followed her, hesitated. "I said slow, remember?"

"Yeah, I remember." But then she reached into his pocket, pulled out the keys, then unlocked the front door. "However, *I* didn't say slow. Come inside and kiss me, Finn." She pushed it open and spun around to face him. "But *this* time, kiss me all over."

His need was a red haze in the back of his eyes. His desire warred with the need to protect her.

Shan stepped inside, heels hitting the floor, her hands coming to the buttons of her coat.

One undone.

The next.

It landed with a whisper of sound next to her heels.

She reached for the zipper on the side of her dress.

And Finn stopped watching.

He moved.

Across the floor, kicking the door shut behind him, pausing the barest second to flip the lock, then he was striding toward Shan, scooping her up into his arms and carrying her down the hall.

Her breath was hot against his throat for the barest second before her tongue flicked out, caressing his skin, lips pressing, teeth nipping and making him jump and groan. Fingers fisting in his hair, her breasts against his chest. He prowled through his room, dumped her onto the bed, and followed her down.

"You are so fucking beautiful," he said and then, because her lips were there and so fucking tempting, he kissed her.

Had just kissing a woman ever been this good?

Never.

Otherwise he would have never stopped doing it.

With Shannon, everything was more intense, evoked bigger emotions, everything was just . . . more.

Her hands slid from his nape, down his spine, nails digging in, and somehow his cock got even harder. He shifted, leaning back so he could trail a hand up her leg, reveling in the silky skin, liking it too much when she wrapped it around his hips.

"Finn," she groaned when his hand continued its movements, tracing up her side, finding the hidden zipper beneath her arm and tugging it down.

She released him long enough to slip her arms free from the straps of her dress then reached for him again, one hand yanking at the bottom of his shirt, the other tugging at the tie around his neck. Yeah. Her using that strip of fabric to haul him closer, to angle his neck until his mouth reached hers was every bit as good as he'd imagined that morning on the deck.

But he wanted to be naked more.

So, he kissed her until his lungs screamed for oxygen, then he pulled back and ripped off his tie, made quick work of the buttons on his shirt before tossing it aside. His shoes hit the floor, followed by his socks and slacks. Then he turned back and . . . nearly swallowed his tongue.

While he'd been undressing, Shannon had one-upped him.

Her dress was off, crumpled to the side, and she was reaching for the clasp of a lacy black bra.

"Wait," he said, snagging her hands, tugging them to her sides, wanting—no—*needing* to look. He didn't know how he was able to function with all of the golden skin on display, the lights overhead showcasing every single curve and silken inch of her. "Fuck, Blue Eyes. You take my breath away."

"Finn," she whispered. "Please, come down here and stop staring at me."

"You're beautiful," he said.

She blushed.

"Truly beautiful."

"Stop." But then she tugged him down on top of her, wrapped her legs around his waist, and kissed him. He turned himself over to the moment, knowing that he would have time to convince her to see her own beauty, that she'd grown leaps and bounds in confidence on her own over the last weeks, that the strength and self-assurance would continue to grow as time went on.

Her hand slipped down, under the waistband of his boxers and, yeah, *that* wasn't happening, not if he wanted to last longer than a teenage boy.

He snagged her wrist, brought it to his mouth, flicked his tongue out. "Fuck, you taste good." Then he reached for the cup of her bra, tugged it down, and nearly came from the sight of those dusky nipples, the soft globes of her breasts exposed and waiting for his mouth. She released a shaky breath, nipples tightening, and he bent, sucked one deep, reveling in her groan, the way she writhed against him, the sweetness of her skin on his tongue.

Fingers in his hair, nails biting against his scalp.

Moans in his ears.

He moved, kissing his way to the other side, nipping and soothing his way over her other breast, tracing her nipple with his tongue. She bucked, fingers tightening, and then he tugged himself loose, traced his mouth along her skin as he moved down and down and *in between.*

Lace torn and tossed to the side. Her labia parted to reveal the glistening, pink folds of her pussy, making his tongue ache, his mouth water, his cock harden to granite.

"Finn—"

She broke off on a long, loud groan when he pressed his lips to her and got to work.

Testing strokes to see what made her writhe, finding the right pressure, circling and dancing his tongue against her clit, falling into the rhythm that had her moaning as she catapulted up and over the edge of pleasure.

"Right—" She broke off. "No—" She reached down and tilted his head slightly to the side. "*There.*"

Never let it be said, he couldn't take direction.

He stayed *there*. He stayed focused, using his tongue, his thumb, slipping a finger inside and working her pussy until he felt her stiffen beneath him, those hands coming back to his head, gripping his hair tight.

"Oh fuck," she groaned and came apart on his tongue.

He ground his hips into the mattress, trying to control the raging need boiling inside him, trying to keep his promise that this night was for her, for slow, and slow didn't include crawling up her body and planting himself deep inside her hot, wet pussy.

Not tonight. Not tonight. Not—

She released his hair, shoved him back, and crawled on top of him.

"Shan—"

"Shh."

There was a crinkle and he glanced down to see she had produced a condom from somewhere. But before he could ask her how or tell her they didn't need to do this tonight, the plastic square was torn open and she was rolling the latex sheath down his cock.

Just the feel of her fingers on him, the last of her still on his tongue, was enough that he almost came right then and there.

"Now, honey," she murmured, "yeah?"

He nodded, unable to form words with her poised above him, eyes hot, pussy . . . so . . . damned . . . close.

Her hips dropped and she took him inside.

Fucking hell.

No. Fucking *heaven*.

His eyes rolled back as she slid down the length of him, taking him until he bottomed out inside her, pussy clenching tightly around him.

She rocked against him. "Finn. I—mmm—I need—"

He moved, flipping them over, lifting one thigh and wrapping it around his waist as he slid in and out, in and out. As he moved faster, deeper, harder. It was too fast. Too hard. Too deep. He knew he should slow down, even as flames licked up his spine, need coiling in his abdomen, the red haze expanding and covering his vision. His orgasm was close. *Too* close.

But then Shannon wrapped her other leg around him, tilting her pelvis, taking him deeper, moaning his name. "More," she gasped when he hit just the right spot. "Right there. *Oh God.*"

Her head flew back, her pussy clenched around his cock, and—

She moaned as she flew over the edge again.

And he lost his battle with slow, pounding into her faster and faster until he exploded, until he lost himself to the most powerful orgasm of his life.

His heart was racing, sweat was dripping down his spine, and his head spun, but he still managed to not collapse on top of Shan, to roll to the side and tug her close instead, then to ask, "Where did you hide that condom?"

Not that.

He'd meant to talk about how great this was, how much she meant, how he'd somehow fallen for this woman in no time at all, and yet it meant more than any other relationship he'd ever had.

Shan laughed, head tilting, eyes finding his, lips curved and so gorgeous that she took his breath away, all over again. "I'll tell you another time."

He grinned, kissed her.

Then he held her tight and let his eyes drift closed.

Just for a few minutes.

SEVENTEEN

TRUCKS AND MORNING WOOD

Shannon

SHE STARTED to roll over but found herself pressed to the mattress by a heavy arm and leg.

A heavy, *male* arm and leg.

Her pulse raced for a moment before she remembered Finn. The glorious night with him. The message from his sister telling them she was going to crash on Shannon's couch and not to feel like they had to rush back.

Which had ended up with them definitely not rushing back home.

It had also ended with them breaking into Finn's condom supply rather than hers.

Three times in one night. That must be a record. A *movie star* record.

She grinned, stifling a giggle since that movie star was currently snoring softly in her ear.

All the agents and publicists in the world couldn't take that out of a man.

She shifted, wincing slightly—because three times. Worth it, for sure. But also, her body wasn't exactly primed and ready to go after her failed marriage. It was certainly primed and ready to go *now*, though.

Finn held her tightly, his warmth having led her to kick off the blankets, his stubble catching her hair, the spicy, male scent of him surrounding her.

Round four, despite the soreness, sounded very appealing.

She sighed, pressed lightly against his chest. Before round four, however, she needed the bathroom, to brush her teeth, and to check her phone to make sure all was good with Ry.

It was still dark outside, the first rays of the morning just barely peeking over the horizon to warm the sky from black to navy, so Rylie wouldn't be awake yet, especially after the excitement of the night before. Plus, Shannon had purposely turned off the Do Not Disturb, just in case Lexy had needed to reach her.

No calls or texts had come through.

So, she felt safe in a bathroom, teeth, check cell, then round four game plan.

But she had to wriggle her way out of Finn's octopus limbs first.

She stifled a giggle when she slipped a leg free, only to have him roll over and pin her to the mattress, his hand sliding up into her hair and weaving into the locks there. His hips inched forward and . . . *hello*, morning wood.

Maybe round four would happen first.

That thought had the stifled giggle emerging.

Finn ran his jaw along hers. "Mornin'," he murmured.

"Morn—"

He kissed her. Shan froze for a millisecond—because hello, morning *breath*—but then his tongue slipped between her lips and she wasn't thinking of her probable dragon breath. She was kissing Finn, and the spicy, intoxicating taste of him was just as good in the morning as it was any other time of day.

Luckily, he seemed to feel the same way about her since the kiss went on long enough to steal all the air from her lungs, leaving her gasping and her pulse thundering in her veins.

"Morning," she said once she could summon enough oxygen to force out the word.

He grinned, brushed his lips over the tip of her nose. "Morning, Blue Eyes," he said, his voice no longer sleepy, hand dropping to her hip, fingertips tracing tiny circles. He pressed one more kiss to her lips then pulled back. "We should get to Rylie."

"That."

She didn't realize she'd spoken aloud until his brows drew together.

"That?"

Shan's first instinct was to deflect, to pull back, to get up and use the bathroom and rush back to her daughter. But . . .

She'd lived a long time hiding who she was.

She was done with that.

They'd spent nearly every day together for more than a month, and Finn, *well*, he'd taken absolutely everything she'd thrown at him, all the little scary pieces she'd been afraid to share, vulnerabilities she'd been terrified to put out there, he'd treated them carefully. He'd protected and sheltered and treaded carefully.

A month might seem like too little time.

But he'd proven himself time and time and *time* again.

"Finn," she said. "I—"

Her words were cut off by the loud rumble of a truck, its almost ear-piercing engine noise breaking the early morning silence.

"What?" Finn pushed out of bed, slipped out into the hall.

They had a road that backed up to the row of beach

cottages, but it was beyond quiet, narrow, and hard to navigate big vehicles on it. Even the UPS truck only came down if there was a package that was too heavy to carry . . . or a multitude of boxes to collect.

Her stomach twisted into knots.

She had no reason to feel this way, but a sinking sensation crept into her gut, and she followed Finn out of bed, rushing down the hallway to peek through the blinds next to him.

A moving truck.

Parking behind *her* house.

What the fuck?

She watched another car pull behind the truck, saw a trio of shadowy figures make their way down the concrete path that led to her door, and her throat seized up.

She turned, rushed back to the bedroom, searching for her clothes, but Finn was already there and ahead of her. He tossed a pair of pajama bottoms, a T-shirt, and a sweatshirt on the bed.

"Get dressed."

Then he grabbed clothes for himself, yanking them on and grabbing their cells.

"Come on."

They rushed to the front door, pushed out it, ran for her deck, and—

Brian.

Fucking Brian.

"What are you doing?" she exclaimed, eyeing the two boys who looked to be college age standing behind him.

He crossed his arms. "The house sold. It closes today. You need to be out."

There was a multitude of problems with his words.

But all she could summon was silence.

Because she was trying to process what in the ever-loving fuck her asshole of an ex was saying.

Then his words hit home, and her heart convulsed.

Then the anger hit.

"You're fucking kidding me," she snapped, clenching her hands into fists. "Please, tell me that you're not fucking serious. That you didn't promise me this house for our *daughter* and then sold it out from beneath me. That you didn't ignore our settlement or my requests or my fucking *lawyer* and do this."

He rolled his eyes, made a noise of disgust. "Don't be dramatic."

"Don't be—" Her hands twitched with the urge to punch him.

"Who's this?" Brian's gaze drifted over her shoulder.

She shook her head. He was telling her he'd taken away her daughter's home, and he was concerned about the man standing at her back. "How was I stupid enough to waste so many years with you?"

"How was I stupid enough to waste so many years with such a dumb bitch?" Brian countered.

"Don't call her that." She felt Finn take a step closer, his chest brushing her back.

Brian rolled his eyes.

"You would do this to our daughter?" she asked. "Show up out of the blue on a Sunday morning? Where are we supposed to go?"

He shrugged. "I'm sure Pepper will let you stay with her."

"And our stuff? What about Rylie's things?"

Another shrug. "They're here to pack up for you. It'll go to a storage unit, and you can retrieve it when you're ready." He pulled out a piece of paper, shoving it at her so she had no choice but to take it. "Your half of the sale, minus the moving fees and six months of storage charges."

Anger swept through her, and she sucked in a breath, biting her tongue until it bled.

"We're done here." Brian turned away from her, took a key out from his pocket, and handed it to the movers. "You're parked in front of the correct house? 5421 Oceanfront?"

Finn stiffened behind her.

The mover nodded, took the keys.

"Brian," she gritted out. "You need—"

"Wait," Finn murmured into her ear. "Just wait for one second. I'll be right back."

He disappeared, footsteps quiet on the deck. Shan heard him, heard his words, but she was more focused on Brian. On the movers.

"She can take until the end of the day," Brian said, as though he were giving her the greatest courtesy.

"Brian," she said.

He turned away, headed for the steps.

"*Brian!*"

"Hash it out with your lawyer," he said. "Or better yet, deposit the check and shut up for once in your life."

He walked around the corner of the house, his footsteps loud in the still quiet morning. She heard his car door slam, the engine start, sand kick up against the undercarriage as he drove away.

The mover cleared his throat, moved as though to unlock the front door.

"Take one step into my house and—"

"It's *my* house, actually."

Finn's voice made her jump and turn around. He had a folder of papers. "I purchased this place several weeks ago. Here's the paperwork"—he extended a thick packet toward the mover—"It's all there. I can call whoever it is that you need in order to verify I made the purchase."

The movers looked at one another. "Do you want her stuff moved?" one asked Finn.

"No."

"Are we still getting paid?" asked the other.

"Yeah. In fact," Finn said and pulled out his wallet, extracting a few bills, "buy yourselves some breakfast, call it an early day, and get on with your weekend."

They looked at each other again, nodded.

"Cool," the first one said. "But if our boss—"

"I'll let your boss know."

The second one blew out a breath. "That'd be great, dude. I can't lose another job, otherwise my mom said I would have to move out."

"Can't have that," Finn deadpanned.

"Nope."

More looking. More standing around.

"You can go," Finn said.

They nodded, started for the stairs then stopped. "Are you Finn Stoneman?"

"Yeah."

"Can we get a selfie?"

"Not today, boys," he said, "Catch me in town sometime for it, okay?"

"Okay."

They waited.

"You can still go."

They shook themselves. "Oh . . . yeah. Okay . . . see you around." With that, they disappeared around the corner and she listened to *their* doors slam, *their* truck engine start up, sand in the undercarriage as they backed slowly down the street.

When it was quiet, she turned to face Finn.

"You bought my house?"

The sun was coming up, highlighting the chagrin in his expression. "I didn't mean to," he said quickly, setting the papers on the table and coming over to her. "I knew that I wanted to spend more time here, more time with you, and so I had my assistant buy me a house."

There were several things wrong with that statement, but probably the biggest one was, "You bought a house without seeing it?"

His gaze dropped to his feet. "I . . . uh . . . yes?"

"Is that a question or an answer?"

A beat then, "An answer."

"Have you done this buying-a-house-without-seeing-it thing before?"

He made a face.

"Oh my God," she exclaimed. "That's a yes. How many times?"

A sigh. "Three? No, with this one, four."

"*Four?*" And she didn't know if she was more shocked by the fact that he had four houses or that he'd *bought* four houses without looking at them.

"I mean, normally I see pictures," he said quickly. "But I liked the town so much. I liked you and Ry so much, that I told him I didn't care about the inside or outside so long as it was on this beach."

She shook her head. "That's why the sign was down," she said. "I thought Brian came to his senses, that Alberto had worked some magic with him, but of course, he didn't. Brian's not capable of sense and Alberto would have called me back with news if he had any." She rubbed her temples. Fuck, what a mess. She'd have to move after all. Luckily, she didn't think Finn would make her do it today, but—

"I'll call today and take care of it."

"Take care of what?" she asked.

"Selling you the house back."

Relief before her heart sank deeper. She couldn't afford to buy the house back, even with the check in her pocket, she wasn't sure if she'd be able to qualify for a big enough mortgage without Brian's income on the application.

"Finn."

"When will the divorce be final?"

"Before all this?" She was doing some mental calculations, trying to figure out if she could pull money out of her retirement in order to borrow a smaller amount. "We'd reached the settlement already, waited the processing time, were just waiting for the papers to come through, but I got the call they were ready yesterday."

"Call your lawyer and sign them."

She frowned, still figuring out numbers even as her gut sank with the reality that there would be absolutely no way she could afford to pay market value for her place. "I'm planning on it."

"Do it today," Finn said. "Cut the tie."

Her eyes shot up. "I don't like your tone, Finn Stoneman."

"Just be done with your ex already. Move on. Move forward."

"What *is* your problem?" she snapped, glaring at him. "You somehow bought my house without me knowing and I'm trying to figure out how I could possibly afford to buy it back. Which I don't think is possible, so I'll need to move anyway. And *further* that, you haven't once given me orders, so I'm not going to let you start doing that today, of all days."

He smiled. "*There* you are, Blue Eyes."

Her teeth clicked together. "What?"

"I was worried there for a second." He closed the distance between them, pulled her close. "I know you've had a lot of promises from the men in your life, but please believe this one." His eyes locked with hers. "I'm not going to screw you over. This house is yours. I wouldn't take it from you. Not now. Not ever."

"But I can't afford to pay market value—"

"You can't afford the price of one batch of peanut butter milk?"

"What?"

"Or for a dollar or whatever minimum amount we need to make it legal?"

"Finn—"

"I don't need the money. I'll keep renting the house next door or buy another place. I don't need this one, and I definitely don't need market value." He cupped her cheek. "I have enough, baby. I don't need this, too."

She sighed, pulled back. "Finn, I can't let you give me this house."

"How about you just give me you, and we'll call it even?"

Her breath froze in her lungs.

"Sign the divorce papers," he said. "And pick me, instead. Let me be the one in your life. Let me be the one who walks with you and Rylie to school. Let me be a part of your lives, and that's all the payment I need."

"Finn—"

"I've had the happiest days of my life here. With you and Rylie. I feel again. I know you better than any woman I've dated, no matter the duration, and you know me just as much. I know everything won't be smooth sailing, and it'll be hard when I'm filming, but I can plan my schedule for more time off." He brushed her hair off her forehead. "I can travel less, stay out of the public eye more so the media attention drops off. I can change my life so that it fits in better with yours and Rylie's. I—"

"I don't want you to change."

He blinked, worry creeping into his expression.

"I love you. I know we've had this ideal sequestered time here. I know things will get harder if and when the media shows up." She took a breath. "But I also know that I *know* you better than I ever knew my husband. You're sweet and funny and kind and . . . you're everything I could have ever dreamed of in a man." Her lips curved. "Even if you are missing those thirty pounds of muscle."

His mouth dropped open.

She gently tipped it closed. "I'm kidding about the muscle," she said. "But I'm not kidding about loving you. I thought I would be alone forever, and then you just came knocking on my door with a bucket of sand toys, and how could I not fall for you?"

"Blue Eyes," he said. "What am I going to do with you?"

"What do you mean?" A spike of nerves. Was it too soon? Of course, it was too soon. She was an idiot and—

"I've been waiting for the right moment to tell you I love you, working it up in this big speech, so you'd hear everything else and not just that and get scared off, and then you just . . . beat me to the punch." His lips twitched. "Now, I have to be the loser who just goes, blah, blah, blah, I love you, too."

She grinned. "You love me?"

A nod. "I never stood a chance otherwise." He picked up her hand, placed it on his chest so she could feel his heart thundering beneath her palm. "I love you, Shannon Torres."

"You know," she said softly, "I grew up watching fairy tales and princess stories but never seeing myself reflected in them. I never saw the brown girl get the blond, white hero. She was always the funny friend or the smart girl in school or the one with the strict parents who never let her do anything." She touched his jaw with one finger. "No one ever told *my* story, and I certainly never saw anything close, and a part of me never believed I could find what I needed and deserved. I never believed I could find *you*."

He covered her hand with his, pressing it flat to his jaw. "Yours is a story that *deserves* to be told. Little girls who look like you, who look like Rylie, should believe they can get the hero, or better yet, that they can *be* the hero."

"And *that's* why I love you."

He kissed her briefly. "Not because I have the money and connections to get those types of stories told?"

A shrug. "Okay, only partly."

Finn laughed and tugged her even closer. "You sign the divorce papers. I'll sign the house papers," he said. "And then we'll keep building this between us. We'll go slow—"

"What if I don't *want* to go slow?"

His mouth fell open again.

She laughed. "I found my gorgeous hero," she said. "Why would I possibly want to go slow?"

"Because I'm still missing those thirty pounds of muscle."

Her mouth dropped open, and then they were both laughing, pressed so tightly together, she forgot, for a moment, where she ended and he began. Or maybe, that was because the laughter abruptly stopped, and Finn slanted his lips across hers, kissing her until her lungs threatened to burst.

A commotion behind them as Rylie burst out the front door and onto the deck. "You're kissing my mom again, Mr. Finn!"

Finn pulled away on a chuckle. "I *am* kissing her," he said. "But I'm also loving her." He squatted down next to Rylie and tucked a strand of her messy bedhead hair behind her ear. "Would it be okay if I love you, too?"

Wide eyes.

Trembling lips.

Then Rylie launched herself into his arms, knocking him back onto his butt on the deck. But Finn had her, his arms wrapped tightly around Ry so she didn't fall.

And Shan knew then that Finn would *always* have them.

Just as she and Ry had him right back.

"I love you, too, Finn," Ry said, squeezing with all of her little might.

"Got room for one more?" Shan asked after a few moments.

Finn's warm, honey eyes met hers, his face soft, his arm lifting automatically, just as she'd known it would because she was already sinking down next to the two people she loved most in the world.

Holding tight.

Being held right back.

Now *that* was the best part of getting the hero.

Well, that, the happy ending, *and* the thirty pounds of muscle.

EPILOGUE

BLUE EYES, WIDE EYES

Finn, Six Months Later

THE NOISE WAS ALMOST DEAFENING inside the small kitchen.

But then again, it *was* Sunday, and this was his family—no, this was *their* family. Because, of course, his parents had loved Shannon and Rylie from their first meeting almost six months before. His sister had dished on Finn being head over heels, and his parents had taken the next plane out, and Finn had found himself temporarily transplanted from the rental into Shannon's house. Of course, it was a temporary he'd finagled his way into making a permanent after his parents had gone home the first time, and it was one he certainly didn't begrudge.

Him and his girls.

Who were wonderful and loving and sweet and just made his life so much *more*.

So, no, it wasn't a surprise they had fit right in with his family.

All of his family. *All* of whom had decided to come visit at the same time, and all of whom were currently creating the nearly deafening noise in Shannon's kitchen.

Add in his mom being a mother hen, who liked to have all of her little chicks close—biologically related to her or not—and his dad having fulfilled a fatherly role to more than a number of his and his siblings' friends and spouses over the years, and Shannon and Rylie were tucked right into the Stoneman fold.

"Sandcastles!" Rylie yelled, running through the fray, his two nieces, Stephanie and Colby, trailing after her like the trio of Musketeers they were. There was clattering as they picked up their swords—er, shovels—from the basket on the deck then pounding footsteps as they sprinted across the wooden planks. His nephews—Max, Mike, Joey, and Teddy—were involved in a very complicated imaginary game on the sand just in front of the house that involved explosions, mobs of bad guys, and copious amounts of digging.

"I should watch them—" Shannon turned to follow the girls.

"I've got them," his dad said, "these old ears need a break from the noise."

He disappeared out the front door.

"Just saying," Lexy said into the beat of quiet that trailed him, one that was punctuated with more cries and orders of "wet sand!" and "five turrets" and "dig faster." Her lips twitched. "I don't think it's any louder in here than out there."

"Accurate," Phil, his younger brother, said, dipping a finger into the sauce their mom was making and earning himself a smack on the hand for his transgression.

"Fingers to yourself, buster!" she snapped, spinning back to the stove.

Lexy bit her lip. "Ooh, you got in trouble!"

His older brother, Steve, snorted, opening the door to pull out a beer, asking the room at large, "Anyone want one?"

Kathy ignored him and asked, "What, are you, six?"

"*Twenty*-six," Lexy retorted.

Shannon said, "I'll take one," completely unperturbed that his family was crowded into her kitchen, that his mom was at her stove, that his brother was helping himself to beverages from her fridge.

Steve passed one over, grinned at her. "You're too good for this brood."

She started to shake her head, his woman who was bright and happy, but who still didn't always see how wonderful she was, and Finn tugged her back against his chest, pressed a kiss to her head. "She *is* too good"—he nuzzled her throat—"She's also too good to say otherwise."

"Finn! I—" A firm shake. "No—"

"Tell me about this peanut butter milk Stephanie was waxing poetic about earlier," Kathy said, rescuing her.

"Well . . ." She started giving away her trade secrets, because she was always generous with her time and knowledge. Finn admitted he began tuning out, letting her voice wash over him, just thrilled to be here with her, to have his family around. He'd be gone for six weeks of shooting in less than a week, and he wanted to soak up every minute.

Such a change.

Half a year ago, he'd been equal parts numb and angry, taking no joy in anything, and today he couldn't care less about the conversation, about the food. The only thing that mattered was . . . family, love, connection.

"Marry me," he blurted.

Of course, he'd unknowingly timed his words to come right during a lull in the conversation, where typically the statement would have been lost in the chatter. Instead, it fell directly into silence.

Shannon twisted in his arms, eyes wide.

"Um, what?" Lexy asked.

"That had better not be your actual proposal, Finn Stone-man," his mother snapped, turning to glare at him, the large wooden spoon held aloft in her hand.

"Shh," Kathy said. "She hasn't answered him yet."

He heard them, obliquely anyway. Because his eyes were on the woman in front of him, the woman whom he loved beyond measure. The woman . . . who was looking at him incredulously.

"What do you say, Blue Eyes?" he asked softly. "Will you make an honest man out of me?"

Her lips slowly curved up, and the impact of her smile was a meteor to his chest. Not a single trace of sad, just pure unadul-terated happy and bright and . . . *love*. Her smile was filled with love. She took a step forward, their toes touching, and reached up to cup his jaw. "You sure about this?"

He scoffed. "Am I sure about the two people I love most in the world?"

"Hey!" Lexy said.

"Shh," Steven hissed.

Shan giggled.

"I love you, baby," he said, covering her hand with his. "But I don't need an answer now. We can wait until this sideshow goes and we're alone—"

"Oh no, you can't!" his mom exclaimed.

More giggles from Shannon.

"Yes, you can," he told her.

"I love you," she said, drifting closer.

"I love you."

"I will marry you"—a burst of noise from his family had her lifting her voice—"but I have *one* condition."

They quieted and Finn's heart skipped a beat, and he hoped, sent a mental prayer out to the universe that he would be able to fulfill that condition, even as he said, "Anything, honey."

Another smile.

This time, one with warmth and love and . . . mischief.

"I'll marry you, but only if you . . . give me those thirty pounds."

"Thirty pounds?" his mom exclaimed. "Thirty pounds of what?"

He burst out laughing. "I'll get on it."

Her chest came flush to his, her other arm wrapped around his shoulders, her lips moving very close to his. "See that you do." And then laughing, she touched her mouth to his, her whispered, "Yes," exhaled against his lips.

He banded his arms around her, held her tight, and forgot all about his family as he kissed the love of his life.

At least until footsteps pounded against the floor.

Until a groan came and a "Mr. Finn. Again?"

Shannon pulled away, still laughing, and squatted in front of her daughter, tugging her close and hugging her tight. "Still with the Mr. Finn, huh?"

"I like it."

"Would you like to maybe call him Dad?" Shan asked, pulling back slightly, cupping her daughter's cheek in her palm.

His lungs froze, his heart squeezed. "It's okay if you don't want—"

Wide eyes turned to his.

"You'll stay?"

"Yes," he said, kneeling down next to Shannon and Ry.

"Forever?"

Finn nodded. "Yes." He was ready when she launched herself at him this time, arms catching her and bringing her close, hugging this little girl, who was wonderful in her own right, tight. "I love you, Ms. Ry."

Her whisper just reached his ears. "I love you, Mr.—" She squeezed him back. "I love you, too, *Dad*."

And kneeling there on the kitchen tile, one arm around this

little girl, his other wrapped around the woman he loved, so much happy and bright and love filling him and this space surrounding them and . . .

Finn lost his heart all over again.

But that was okay.

Because his girls had him.

And they weren't letting go.

Shannon, A Year Later

She was wearing a fancy dress and big ol' heels.

But that wasn't the most surreal thing.

No, the most surreal thing was that she'd gotten used to the flashes of lights, used to the red carpet, used to the cameras occasionally being pointed in her direction, used to the odd story here or there on the gossip sites.

It hadn't been the odd story at first.

For a while, after news of their small wedding had broken, it had been *all* the stories.

But Stoneybrook was still their safe place.

The odd paparazzo found their way into town now and then, but Stoneybrook's residents always pulled rank, tightened their inner circle, and froze the photographers out. They quickly found out that the long trip to town wasn't worth the mediocre pictures.

Time had passed.

The media had moved on to the next story.

Finn still left to film movies, though he'd lightened his promotion and shooting schedule considerably so he could spend more time with his girls. Shan still taught third grade, and Rylie was now in second grade—well, almost *done* with second.

And to celebrate the end of another school year, as well as some expensive lawyering—*cough*, movie star perks—Finn had formally adopted Ry.

So, things were the same.

And yet, so, *so* different.

They were a family. They'd been welcomed by Finn's parents and siblings. They had ties and connections and a house that was often loud and full to bursting with people and voices and love. And . . . Shan had piles of textbooks at home, online courses in progress, now knowing that while she still wanted to work with kids, instead of being solely in the classroom, she wanted to focus more on educational intervention and social support. She wanted to help the kids who were falling behind, wanted to stop them from slipping between the cracks.

It paid even less than being a teacher.

But funny how being married to a movie star made that less of a worry. *Ha.*

Looking decent in front of a bunch of flashbulbs while six months pregnant, on the other hand, was a bigger one.

"Shannon!"

"Look here!"

"Shan!"

Thankfully, she'd practiced for this moment. She'd gotten the posing tips, her hair done, her dress from a designer and yet, underneath it all, she was just a normal mom. Maybe she had never fit in with the rail-thin, blonde-beauty princesses in all the fairy tales she'd yearned for, but now she didn't mind that her hair was dark, that she was very far away from those skinny, fictional stereotypes.

She had her happy ending.

She didn't need to fit into a story or a film or—

"Blue Eyes."

A shiver skated down her spine.

Despite the calls of her name, she'd been hanging to the side, letting the big stars do the heavy lifting of photo-call. This movie may have been inspired partly by Shannon's life, partly by a book Lexy had given Finn on her first visit to Stoneybrooke, but this film was really just an ode to all the women who weren't "typical" heroines. And the driving force to get it made, the one who'd had the vision for the project in the first place, the one who'd given a lot of the money, and *definitely* the one who'd devoted an almost endless amount of hours into finding people who could carry out that vision had been Finn.

He'd heard her talk about the princesses and storylines.

He'd heard her talk about how she felt different and less.

He'd heard her talk about how she'd never seen people who looked like her on screen growing up, and he didn't want Rylie, didn't want other boys and girls *like* Rylie to have that experience.

So, *this*.

Lending his name but taking a backseat in acting and directing. Funding different stories by different authors. Finding people with like minds to work with, to act in, to direct and produce who may not have otherwise had the opportunity.

"Ready to go?" he asked, pulling her into the present by cupping her cheek, staring down at her like there weren't a million cameras pointed at them and flashbulbs going off.

She smiled at her husband, staring up at the love of her life, who'd come and found her on the sidelines, who'd never put her there, who would never let her stay there, even if she put *herself* there. He would always find her, would always protect and cherish her.

And *that* was everything she'd ever dreamed about.

That was her happily ever after.

"Yeah, baby," she murmured.

He brushed a kiss over her forehead, leaned down to whisper in her ear, "Let's go home."

She nodded, let her body drift toward his. "Yes," she murmured. "You've *finally* given me those promised thirty pounds"—he'd just finished filming a flick in a popular superhero franchise and had bulked up for it—"I need to take advantage of it."

Just as she'd expected when bringing up their private joke, Finn started laughing, warm honey eyes on hers, one hand still resting on her cheek, the other dropping to her belly.

She rose on tiptoe, pressed her lips to his.

Flashes went off.

She'd had her press lessons. She'd practiced and prepped. She'd studied up.

And because of that, Shannon knew *this* was the shot that would be everywhere tomorrow.

She dropped back to her heels, the love in his eyes feeding her soul, filling her heart. Yeah, she could live with that, with this man loving her.

And with the thirty pounds.

Rob

It was probably a morbid birthday tradition for him to be in a graveyard, a beer at his hip, a bouquet of daisies laid across his late wife's headstone.

But . . . the daisies had been her favorite.

Well, the beer had been her favorite, too.

His best friend, his buddy, his love. Carmella had watched more sports than him, had gotten him turned onto IPAs, had dished shit his way more than anyone else. And . . . he'd loved her more than anything.

But now she was gone, and he was sitting in the graveyard on his birthday, because it was something to do when his life was filled with absolutely nothing.

Cool.

Super positive outlook you have there.

The mental voice was Carmella's, and it was no surprise she was giving him shit from the other side of the grave.

He just wished she was around to give it in person.

That wasn't to be, of course.

And it was time he stopped grieving. Or if not that, then it was time he stopped hanging around in the graveyard. Because he'd had enough beers to admit that he'd spent more than just his birthday here.

A lot more.

Stop moping, Rob.

Sighing, he collected his empties and stood, slightly wavering because the bottles numbered four, but that was okay because Stoneybrook was a small ass town and his house was all of two blocks away.

He weaved his way through the graves, dumped the bottles in the trash can near the exit, and started walking along the road.

It was dark, nearing midnight, with only the moon to light his way.

But again, that was okay. Because he'd done this walk more times than he could count.

The town was quiet, having rolled up its streets hours before.

So, the last thing Rob expected was the car.

He'd just stepped out of the shadows across the road from

his house when he saw the headlights . . . coming right toward him.

He froze.

This was it. This was when his loneliness would end, when he would finally see Carmella again. *Finally.*

The car screeched to a halt.

Inches from him. Close enough he could feel the heat of the engine, hear the ticking of the metal parts inside the transmission.

Then the door flew open, and he saw heels appear on the street. High, *high* heels Carmella would never wear. Bare ankles, calves, and knees appeared and then a glimpse of thigh encased in a short, tight skirt. Another thing Carmella would never wear.

"What in the fuck do you think you're doing crossing the street without looking in the middle of the night?" the woman yelled.

That was Carmella.

Fierce. Tough.

But *this* wasn't his Carmella. Rob wobbled slightly, the beers catching up with him, even as he had the distinct thought that this woman was. Not. His. Carmella.

"It's my birthday," he muttered.

"I don't give a fuck if it's the pope's birthday—" She broke off.

Probably because right then he bent at the waist and puked all over his own shoes.

He couldn't even summon up the strength to be embarrassed . . . because the moment after his stomach was emptied, the whole world went black.

The last thing he heard was,

"Shit. Motherfucker. Son of a bitch!"

And that made him smile.

Because *that* mouth was his Carmella.

———

THANK YOU FOR READING! I hope you loved meeting Finn and Shannon! The next book in the Life Sucks series is DUMP-STER FIRE. **Rob was single. That hadn't been the plan. Then came a woman who was definitely *not* his late wife...but who might be the possibility of something more...**

CLICK HERE TO READ DUMPSTER FIRE NOW>

The more she falls for Stefan, the more she risks her career... Don't miss the Gold Hockey series. It begins with the over 400 five-star-reviewed BLOCKED!

"Off-the-charts hot, smexy scenes with one of the best book boyfriends I have come across!" —Amazon reviewer

———

I so appreciate your help in spreading the word about my books, including sharing with friends! Please leave a review on your favorite book site!

If you'd like to receive emails from me for new releases and monthly giveaway sign up for my newsletter https://www.elisefaber.com/newsletter.

You can also join my Facebook group, the Fabinators, for exclusive giveaways and sneak peeks of future books!

Hate missing Elise's new releases? Love contests, exclusive excerpts and giveaways?

Then signup for Elise's newsletter here!

https://www.elisefaber.com/newsletter

And join Elise's fan group, the Fabinators (https://www. facebook.com/groups/fabinators) for insider information, sneak peaks at new releases, and fun freebies! Hope to see you there!

LIFE SUCKS SERIES

ALSO BY ELISE FABER

Billionaire's Club (**all stand alone**)

Bad Night Stand

Bad Breakup

Bad Husband

Bad Hookup

Bad Divorce

Bad Fiancé

Bad Boyfriend

Bad Blind Date

Bad Wedding

Bad Engagement

Bad Bridesmaid

Bad Swipe

Bad Girlfriend

Bad Best Friend

Bad Billionaire's Quickies

Gold Hockey (**all stand alone**)

Blocked

Backhand

Boarding

Benched

Breakaway

Breakout

Checked

Coasting

Centered

Charging

Caged

Crashed

A Gold Christmas

Cycled

Caught

Cap

Covered

Breakers Hockey (all stand alone)

Broken

Boldly

Breathless

Ballsy

Rush Hockey

Big Puck Energy

Filthy Puckboy

So Pucking Over It

Love, Pucks, and Other Stories

Love, Action, Camera (all stand alone)

Dotted Line

Action Shot

Close-Up

End Scene

Meet Cute

Love After Midnight (**all stand alone**)

Rum And Notes

Virgin Daiquiri

On The Rocks

Sex On The Seats

Life Sucks Series (**all stand alone**)

Train Wreck

Hot Mess

Dumpster Fire

Clusterf*@k

FUBAR

Roosevelt Ranch Series (**all stand alone, series complete**)

Disaster at Roosevelt Ranch

Heartbreak at Roosevelt Ranch

Collision at Roosevelt Ranch

Regret at Roosevelt Ranch

Desire at Roosevelt Ranch

Phoenix Series (**read in order**)

Phoenix Rising

Dark Phoenix

Phoenix Freed

Phoenix: LexTal Chronicles (**rereleasing soon, stand alone, Phoenix world**)

From Ashes

In Flames

To Smoke

KTS Series (all stand alone, series complete)

Riding The Edge

Crossing The Line

Leveling The Field

Scorching The Earth

Cocky Heroes World

Tattooed Troublemaker

ABOUT THE AUTHOR

USA Today bestselling author, Elise Faber, loves chocolate, Star Wars, Harry Potter, and hockey (the order depending on the day and how well her team -- the Sharks! -- are playing). She and her husband also play as much hockey as they can squeeze into their schedules, so much so that their typical date night is spent on the ice. Elise is the mom to two exuberant boys and lives in Northern California. Connect with her in her Facebook group, the Fabinators or find more information about her books at www.elisefaber.com.

facebook.com/elisefaberauthor

amazon.com/author/elisefaber

bookbub.com/profile/elise-faber

instagram.com/elisefaber

tiktok.com/@elisefaberauthor

goodreads.com/elisefaber